WHAT A GIRL WANTS

DEBBIE IOANNA

BLOODHOUND
— BOOKS —

www.bloodhoundbooks.com

Print ISBN: 978-1-5040-8599-1

To Cleo, my cat, for keeping my feet toasty warm and also slightly punctured during the editing process.

GRADUATION DAY

Charlotte twirled in front of the glass doors, enjoying the reflection of the graduation gown dancing around her legs in the light summer breeze, teasing the hem of the blue floral dress her mum had bought for the occasion. They had spent several of the previous weekends visiting different shopping centres, searching for the perfect dress that would be suitable for the ceremony as well as the celebrations to follow later in the day. She sat the graduation cap on her head, carefully arranging it around her hair, and admired herself again. The day had come at last. The biggest day of her life, so far at least, and she was able to share it with the love of her life on their one-year anniversary.

As she checked once more that her hair was neat and in place, and topped up her make-up, a handsome face appeared alongside hers in the reflection, knocking her cap with his as he rested his head on her shoulder. His black, solidly gelled hair was gently prickling her ears.

"Did I ever tell you how much you look like Snow White when you wear red lipstick?" He turned his head so he could look adoringly into her eyes and her face burned pink as he dipped below the cap and kissed her cheek, not wanting to smudge her lips. "Happy anniversary, babe."

"How are you not nervous?" She watched as he straightened up his cap, ensuring he didn't have a hair out of place, fascinated that he was not showing any signs of anxiety for what was to come. Watching YouTube videos of past graduation ceremonies had been a mistake. Tripping over one's gown had been a common accident that people were willing to upload to the video streaming site.

"Why would I be nervous?" Sam laughed. "This is it! The first day of the rest of our lives. No more exams, no more assignments, or studying or deadlines. We made it." He reached out to calm her fidgety hands. She always picked at her nails when she was anxious.

"But what if I trip and fall?"

"I will be right there to catch you." He placed his hands on her shoulders and squeezed to reassure her. "This is really it though. We've done it. My degree means I can finally get that internship at TeleTec. They're going to be the next Google, it's going to be epic. *Everyone* is after this job, but it's mine, I know it is." His smile was infectious, and Charlotte was soon picturing their perfect future. "Just think, once the internship is done, I'll be taken on properly and earning loads. I'll buy us a great big house to live in. You won't need to get a salaried job, you can become a full-time author straight away. You'll be the next, what's she called that you love?"

"L. Rosebud." Charlotte had just finished reading her latest novel and was still swooning over the ending where Carla and Adam had realised they were soulmates and walked off happily into the sunset to live their lives together at last, as she and Sam were about to.

"That's it! No, you won't be the next L. Rosebud. You will be the first Charlotte Hicks. Or, maybe one day, Charlotte Wallace." He raised an eyebrow, waiting for her reaction.

"Hmm." She smiled. "What are you suggesting, Mr Wallace?" Charlotte felt like she could faint, but was still being held steady by Sam.

"One day, not now, not here, but I *will* propose. It will be magical and perfect and as wonderful as you can imagine. You can have your own fairy tale wedding, like in those books. Or I might be really original and cause a scene with a flash mob proposal in the middle of a bookshop, how about that?"

"Oh, Sam!" She threw her arms around his neck and the tassels on their caps knocked together as a bell rang in the distance.

"That's our cue." He pulled back. "But before we go…" He reached into his gown, navigating his way to his back trouser pocket, and gestured for Charlotte to turn back round. She did as she was told, once again facing her reflection in the glass, when something shimmered in front of her face.

"Oh my!" Charlotte glanced down at the pendant necklace Sam had placed around her neck. The diamond twinkled in the sunlight and on the back of the small silver plate were the words "C&S, Happily Ever After".

"Do you really mean it?" Charlotte asked, feeling like she was living in a dream.

"Of course I do." He smiled. "All I want is to make you happy, and I know that when I get this job, I can do just that."

Sam held out his hand and she grasped it and they each took a deep breath as they psyched themselves up for their graduation ceremony, and the rest of their lives, together, just the two of them.

CHAPTER 1

EIGHT YEARS LATER...

*C*harlotte turned the key and entered her and Sam's ground floor apartment. Shoes clogged the hallway and she kicked them out of the way, telling herself again to order a proper shoe rack from Amazon, knowing full well it was going to be added to the never-ending "when I get paid" list which was getting longer and longer as time went on as the bills became harder and harder to manage.

She pushed the door shut using her foot as her hands were carefully balancing her bags and the mail. Mainly birthday cards, recognisable due to the varying colourful envelopes, all for her to open the next day. She felt sad there were not as many cards as there used to be as friendships had dwindled over the years as people moved on with their lives to more exciting places, never sticking around in their hometown. Somewhere down the line it became more socially acceptable to send a Facebook message instead of forking out a few pounds for a card and a stamp, but you could always rely on those great aunts to send you a little something.

Amongst the birthday cards, bills, takeaway leaflets and junk mail was a parcel, and this made her very excited indeed as she knew what it contained. Charlotte contemplated opening it a day early. After all, she was an adult and there was no one to stop her, but she decided to wait until morning, seeing as though it was a birthday present to herself. There were not many of those anymore either.

"Is that you?" Sam called from the living room.

"Yeah." She ran into the kitchen, dropping her bags on the table and put the mail on the worktop, flicking through the cards, recognising the handwriting of the senders, before she spotted something different. Something far too formal and fancy to be a birthday card. "Do you want a brew?" she asked as she flicked the kettle on, before noticing the state of the kitchen.

"Please."

"Didn't you get chance to clean up today?" It was nearing the end of March and Sam had taken the week off to use the last of his annual leave before the end of the financial year, so Charlotte was instantly annoyed that he hadn't used his time more productively. The sink was overflowing with cups, the dishwasher was nearly full and could easily have been switched on during the day, and a full carton of warm milk was on the counter and not in its rightful place. She crammed some more things into the dishwasher and turned it on, and then picked up a cloth and brushed some crumbs into the bin so the surface was clean. She had kept a few cups out of the dishwasher so she could wash them by hand and, using the now-warm milk, she began to make them both a cup of tea.

"Not yet."

Charlotte stirred their drinks and carried them into the lounge, the mysterious card tucked under her arm. Sam was laid back on his recliner, still wearing the shorts he often slept in and an old T-shirt which was so stretched around his bulging stomach the faded logo was no longer clear. He was engrossed in a game on his Xbox so didn't look up when Charlotte placed his tea down on the coffee table in front of him, or thank her for it.

"What have you been doing today?" She sipped her tea, thinking she could answer that question for him.

He scratched his matted beard. "Not much. You're back early, aren't you?" His eyes still focused on his game.

"No, it's nearly six."

"Is it?" he looked up from his game at her. "That's gone quick."

"Yeah, have you erm, got anything ready for dinner?" she asked even though she knew the answer to that as well seeing as though there was no smell of a delicious home-cooked meal being prepared as she walked in.

"Nah, we can get another takeaway if you want."

Charlotte looked down at her own tummy which was not as flat as it used to be after years of convenience food. The button on her work trousers was pushing painfully into her stomach, urging her to undo them and relieve the pressure, but she decided to hold off until later when she could put her comfortable pyjamas on. She was too embarrassed to order another new, larger pair of trousers from head office again.

She turned her attention back to the mysterious card and began delicately tearing at the envelope to reveal its contents.

"What have you got there?" Sam nodded towards the card that Charlotte had finally opened.

"It's Hema's wedding invitation!" She smiled as she was suddenly caked in golden glitter which fell from the card, feeling excitement for her best friend's upcoming nuptials. "Aw, her and Mark getting married, isn't it exciting? I forgot the invite was on the way, I'll have to call her."

"Yeah, whatever." Sam resumed his game.

"Aw, wow." She swooned as she opened the card. "A Christmas wedding! At the Winter Gardens a few days before Christmas, isn't that romantic?"

"Sure."

"Like she always wanted." Charlotte held the invitation to her chest, still smiling that her best friend was marrying the man she loved after only two years together. She looked over at her boyfriend of nine years, wondering if they would ever get around to tying the knot like they had talked about all those years ago. "You know, weddings don't have to be big affairs."

"Hmm."

Charlotte picked at the skin around her nails which were caked in glitter.

"They can be small, personal events with a handful of people. One or two friends and family. They don't have to cost much either."

"They're always expensive. Even being a guest is expensive." He scratched at his untamed beard again which Charlotte wished he would shave off. "How much is this thing going to cost us?"

"Well…" Charlotte hadn't been completely honest with him until then. "You know I'm a bridesmaid, but Hema's buying the dress so that's fine. But we might need to stay in a hotel so we're not worrying about arranging a taxi, and there'll be the gift, your suit–"

"I have a suit. Sorted."

Charlotte knew it had been a few years since he'd worn it, and it would be a very tight fit. "We can sort that later." She put the invitation back in the envelope. "But I'm saying, if we were ever to, you know, get married…"

"We can't get married, how many times do I have to say?" He finally put his game controller down. "We want to buy a house, don't we? We can't afford to do both. No matter how cheap you reckon it could be, there are always hidden costs."

"But if we…"

"No, not yet." He pulled himself out of the recliner with a heave and walked out of the room. He left his untouched tea on the coffee table and left Charlotte alone, clutching the wedding invitation in her hands. "What are all these?" he stuck his head back in the room.

"My birthday cards, for tomorrow."

"Oh, right. Erm, I'm going for a shower."

It wouldn't be the first year he'd forgotten her birthday.

CHAPTER 2

The spring sunlight was beaming through the bedroom curtains on the morning of Charlotte's birthday and she woke up with a smile listening to the birds singing, imagining they were serenading her with "Happy Birthday". She was glad that her birthday fell on a Saturday this year as it meant she could have a day to herself and not worry about the stresses of a work day.

Being the manager of the local children's nursery kept her terribly busy through the week. Even though the kids and babies were lovely and she had a great team of nursery practitioners around her, she was always working nonstop.

Friday afternoons were her favourite as she always set aside time to sit with the older children so they could listen to her made-up stories. They would all sit around her, completely mesmerised by her magical worlds and the characters that she brought to life. The staff always told her to get these stories written and published, but she never had time for that anymore. The dream of being an author was a thing of the past.

She picked up her phone. It was already full of Facebook notifications wishing her a happy birthday. She clicked "like" on them all and sent the odd thank you in return before checking the weather forecast. It was going to be sunny all day and she was determined to make the most of it for a change.

"What time is it?" Sam asked from beside her.

"Just after eight." She threw the duvet off her and stood to stretch. Being twenty-nine didn't feel much different, she thought happily.

"Why are you getting up? It's early."

"It's going to be a lovely day." She pulled back the curtains to look out and felt a gentle, spring-like breeze from the small vent above the window. There wasn't a cloud in the sky. "We should go for a walk."

"Why?" He winced at the light hitting his eyes.

"Because we never go anywhere." The small communal garden was littered with old chairs covered in cobwebs and plant pots filled with the corpses of failed flora. "The weather is going to be nice, we need to make the most of it, and a birthday outing sounds perfect."

"Birthday? Oh, right. Erm…" He threw the duvet off and put his old shorts from the previous day back on. "Wait there." He stumbled out of the bedroom.

Charlotte suddenly felt excited. Maybe he didn't forget her birthday after all and was bringing in a card and present for her. She wondered what he could have bought her. He'd had the whole week off work so there was plenty of time to plan something exciting. A new bookcase that she'd hinted about, maybe? Or some vouchers to go clothes shopping? Maybe he would surprise her with a weekend away, they hadn't been anywhere together like that in years and they could do with a change of scenery to make their lives a bit more exciting.

As she waited impatiently, she made the bed and tidied the pillows. The wash basket was overflowing so she would make sure to get that in the washing machine soon so it could be hung out before the neighbours got to the washing line first.

After a few minutes, Sam came back in and she pretended not to notice, wondering what he would be surprising her with.

"Here, erm, happy birthday."

She turned full of hope and expectations, to be presented with a cup of tea.

"Aw, thank you." She took the drink and glanced at his other hand which was empty.

"I didn't have chance to get you a card. Erm…" He looked sheepishly around the room. "Let's go for that walk, eh? It sounds good. I'll get myself sorted and we can go." He smiled at her before leaving the room.

"Yeah, okay. I'll get ready too."

She did her best to hide her disappointment as he made his way to the bathroom and turned on the shower. *He spent most of his time messing about on his phone, would it have been too difficult to order me a card online?* she wondered. The tea was pale and barely hot as he'd overdone it with the milk, so she put it to one side to answer her phone which was ringing.

"Happy birthdaaaaaay!"

She tried her best to sound happy. "Thank you, Hema."

"Mum's taking me for my first dress fitting this morning, but I can call in later with your present, what time will you be in?"

"We're going out for a walk soon, but we will be in later on." Charlotte did not have hopes for a meal out somewhere to celebrate that evening.

"Aw, a walk sounds nice! That won't have been Sam's idea, or was it? Is he taking you somewhere romantic? In that case, I wonder… today could be the day!"

"No, I don't think so. You're the only blushing bride this year," she said quietly so there was no chance of Sam overhearing from the bathroom.

"And you're going to be a stunning bridesmaid! I think I've chosen the dresses for you girls, I just need sizes. My mum wants you over ASAP to get measurements. She's altering them herself.

You know what Mrs Patel's like, if she hasn't done them herself you may as well wear a bin bag."

Charlotte was dreading this moment. The other bridesmaids were Hema's sisters and they were all young, stunning slender girls with bodies to die for.

"I'll get back to you on that one." She put her hand to her stomach. "I'm not sure if I'll have time."

Hema knew her friend's concerns. "Please don't worry about sizes. You're going to look fabulous, I promise. My mum will make sure of it. Oh, hang on." She paused. "Talk of the devil, that's my mum calling, she must be outside. I have to go. Have a great walk! Get your shorts on, it's gorgeous out there today, and warm too!"

"I will, have a good day; send me a photo of the dress!"

They ended their call and Charlotte opened her wardrobe to find some suitable clothes to wear. It was too nice for her usual attire of baggy jeans and oversized T-shirt. She dug around in one of the drawers and found her size twelve shorts, feeling surprised that she could get her size fourteen body into them, although the button dug into her slightly. *They'll do for a morning walk*, she thought. They weren't too uncomfortable when standing.

Charlotte checked her phone, which was pinging with messages and notifications wishing her a happy birthday. There was also the obligatory email from Dorothy Perkins, Next and even Music Magpie wishing her the best on her birthday with an added bonus of a ten per cent discount off her next online purchase. At least *they'd* made some effort.

Sam joined her in the kitchen as she was sipping water, not wanting to eat yet in case the waistband of her shorts became too tight. She'd opened her cards and put them on the windowsill and was halfway through opening up her parcel.

"Who's that from?" Sam asked.

She smiled. "From me, just a little treat."

She pulled out the book. *Moonlight Love* by L. Rosebud. Her latest release and Charlotte was excited to get started on it later. She'd pre-ordered it months earlier and was very happy that it was released in time for her birthday. She considered it a personal gift from the author.

"Not another one of those, they're all the same," Sam retorted, pulling his phone out of his pocket. "Girl meets boy, falls in love, something terrible happens so they split but, in the end, realise they're meant to be and boom, happy ever after."

"It's not just that." She often had to defend her love of these books, but it was no use. "They're romantic and filled with love and fantasy. And I've loved her books for years, you know that."

He shrugged. "You can't help what you like. You ready to go?"

"Yeah." She checked over her outfit using her camera phone, suddenly feeling self-conscious in her shorts. It had been a few years since she'd dared to have her legs on show. "Are these shorts okay? Do they make me look fat?"

"No, you look fine." His eyes were now glued to his phone as he scrolled through Facebook.

"You're not even looking." She tapped him on the arm. "Are they all right?" He finally turned to look at her. "Well?"

His pained expression told her all she needed to hear, but he spoke anyway.

"Think you need the next size up."

She looked down, pulling her T-shirt down so it would stretch over her love handles and hide the bulge.

"How could you say that?" She tried but failed to hold back the tears.

"You asked! Are we going or not?"

"No." She sniffed. She didn't feel like going anywhere anymore. "It doesn't matter. I have things to do anyway."

With the new book still in her hands, she turned and walked out of the kitchen, hearing Sam huff at the sudden, inconvenient change of plans. She avoided their bedroom and instead went to the spare room which had become her domain and slammed the door shut behind her. She stood for a few minutes, letting herself cry until her tears slowed, allowing her to focus on her room.

When they'd moved into their apartment eight years earlier, this room was intended to be her writing room. Sam had surprised her with a large desk and state-of-the-art leather swivel chair so she could get on with her plans of being a writer. Her following birthday, he brought home a large bookcase for her to fill with all her favourite reads, and the following Christmas he bought her a grey checked armchair so she could sit and read her books in comfort and peace.

As time went on, the gifts dwindled and the dream of becoming a writer floated away like a balloon in the sky. The desk was now covered with boxes and the armchair filled with a never-ending pile of clothes that needed ironing. Her bookcase was jam packed with books. There was no order to them anymore as there was no room to organise them properly and some of the books were in piles on the floor.

Her eye caught a pair of baggy pyjama bottoms on her chair which she pulled out of the mess and shoved on, throwing her shorts across the room. It knocked one of the boxes on her desk and some clutter fell to the floor.

"Bugger," she said. Not wanting to add to the mess, she bent down to clear everything up. Among the papers were some old photos from their days at university. The one that stood out the most was of her and Sam which she picked up to get a closer look at. They hadn't been together long judging by how loved up they were. They were laid together on a lawn, sunbathing in shorts and vest tops. Sam was wearing one of those bead chains from Topman which were all the rage back then and his hair was spiked, thick with gel. There was no fat on show to be ashamed of. They looked happy. They looked in love.

Charlotte shoved the clothes onto the floor, freeing up her armchair. She curled up, as much as she could, not taking her eyes off the photo still in one hand as she clutched onto the pendant necklace with the other, which she'd not taken off since their graduation day.

"Where did it go wrong?" she asked herself. "Where did *we* go wrong?"

CHAPTER 3

Not wanting her birthday to be a total loss, Charlotte
made a start on reading her new book. Tucked away
in her room, the sound of Sam's frustration at his game kept out
thanks to the thick walls, she found herself lost in a world of love
and passion between two strangers and she longed to be the
heroine who was beautiful and desired by the knight in shining
armour. She'd forgotten how comfortable her armchair was. The
warm spring sun shining on her through the window made her
feel as though she was on a sun lounger on her favourite beach as
she read.

*Henry glanced in Eliza's eyes, passion burning up inside as he
longed to touch her face, only to be stopped by thoughts of his family's
disapproval of their union, which only made their desire for one another
more powerful.*

*"What are we going to do?" Eliza asked. Tears threatened to fall as
she fought against her emotions to remain strong.*

*"I don't know," he said as he stroked her cheek. "I just don't know.
Since meeting you yesterday, I can't stop thinking about you. You're all
I think about, all I want. Eliza, I must..."*

Charlotte jumped as her phone pinged and vibrated on the

wooden desk all at once, annoyingly bringing her from a secluded Greek beach back to her now-gloomy spare room as the sun had disappeared behind some clouds. She placed a bookmark between the pages and picked up her phone, expecting another excitable birthday message she would rather ignore.

What do you want for tea? x

She was frustrated that Sam felt the need to text her rather than knock on the door to see if she was okay. The sun had been shining gloriously all day but it was wasted on her. She hadn't even realised it was approaching 6pm. Her anger at Sam, as well as being lost in her new book, had clearly kept any hunger at bay. As she considered her reply, she glanced at the photo of them again which she'd left on the arm of the chair, and remembered how they would spend their birthdays in the early days. He would always pretend to forget.

No matter how much she laughed and tried, he would stick by the story that he'd forgotten. Then by the evening, as she had her bath, he would be busy decorating their flat with balloons and banners. Drinks would be poured, food in the oven, sometimes her brother and Hema would be there too to celebrate. And the presents, wow. Tickets to Rome, spa weekends, jewellery. She had received some fantastic gifts over the years. Two years previously, the first time it happened, he had genuinely forgotten her birthday. After she had played along with the non-existent joke, he really did seem mortified. This year, though, it was just another day.

She still tried to make an effort with *his* birthdays. This year she had bought him the new trainers he had asked for, as well as a twelve-month Netflix subscription. She had hoped they could cosy up together to watch some boxsets, but he always started them without her.

As she stepped out of her room, she glanced at the doorframe where there was still evidence of Sellotape from when Sam had taped up balloons for one of her birthdays. She wandered into the kitchen. She should have been greeted with Prosecco in glasses, plates ready for freshly cooked food and a cake filled with candles waiting to be lit. Instead, there were cups once again flowing out of the sink, spilled sugar by the kettle and an oven tray covered in melted cheese on top of the cooker which hadn't been there that morning.

She sighed. *I'd best clean up then.*

She opened the Netflix app on her phone so she could watch *The Big Bang Theory* while she loaded the dishwasher and cleaned down the work surface, like she had done the previous night. The packaging from her book was still on the table along with the envelopes from her birthday cards. She scooped them all up together to put in the bin when a leaflet floated from the packaging to the floor.

Meet the author!
As a buyer of a first edition of Moonlight
Love, you are automatically admitted to meet
L. Rosebud at your nearest Waterstones.
L. Rosebud is grateful for the support over
the last fifteen years of writing and will
come to any store where interest is registered
for a one-off book signing.
Register on the website below and enter your
unique serial number to receive your ticket.
Admissions will be limited, don't miss out!

Charlotte couldn't believe what she was reading. She would get the chance to meet her favourite author. Her inspiration. She owned every book L. Rosebud had ever published and now she would finally be able to meet her. This was the birthday surprise she'd needed to perk her up.

Sam walked into the kitchen. He had changed back into his shorts which were now stained with melted cheese. "What are you grinning at?"

"This!" She thrust the leaflet at him, forgetting how annoyed she'd been. "Look! I can meet her! I'll finally be able to meet her and get a book signed. Isn't that exciting?"

"Yeah, whatever." He passed the leaflet back to her. "I'm ordering a pizza, is that all right?"

"That's fine. Will you come with me?"

"To what? To that meeting? No thanks," he scoffed.

"But it could be fun, you love Waterstones."

Whenever she was lost in the aisles and aisles of books, he would be busy looking through the graphic novels he used to collect which were now stuffed away in the back of the wardrobe. He wasn't interested this time though. She couldn't remember the last time he'd gone with her. They used to spend their free days together driving from town to city to village hunting for small, independent bookshops, but not anymore.

"I can go anytime, you don't need me to go with you to that to just stand around waiting for you." He shook his head as pulled out his phone. "Meat feast pizza alright?"

"Yes, if that's what you want."

"Okay," he tapped away on his phone to put their order through, clearly no longer wanting to talk about Charlotte's desired trip to meet her idol.

She typed the web address into the Google app on her own phone and saw that L. Rosebud was already booked to go to her local Waterstones on 15 May. Just two months away. She quickly entered her serial number and within seconds received a confirmation email with her ticket. She let out a squeal of excitement and bounced out into the hallway away from Sam and into their bedroom, determined to pick out the best outfit. An outfit that said; "I am an aspiring author".

She pulled out her smart pin-stripe trousers and pulled down her comfy pants so she could try them on. As she stood in front of the mirror though, she stopped. She looked at herself.

Where did that size ten body go? she wondered. She turned around and observed her body. The elastic of her knickers wasn't visible as her tummy fat had rolled over, covering it up. Thigh gap was a thing of the past and the dimples in her paper-white legs made her uncomfortable. There was no resemblance to the girl in the photo.

"The pizza's on the way," Sam called.

"Okay." It was their second pizza that week, not forgetting the Chinese on Monday. Or the fish and chips on Thursday. Fast food ordered via an app was so convenient, wasn't it?

Sitting together at the kitchen table, Sam was on his fourth slice of pizza as Charlotte was still nibbling on her first, still thinking about how much weight she must have gained over the years. She was too scared to step on her weighing scales, which were gathering dust behind the bathroom sink. She'd always considered going on a diet, but the thought of getting home from work late in the day and preparing a meal for the both of them put her off. She just didn't have the time, or the energy most days.

They had barely spoken since sitting down. Sam had just wanted to eat in the living room as they always did, but Charlotte had insisted on sitting together at the kitchen table for a change.

"Look," Sam began, "I'm sorry."

"What for?" she said, coyly.

"For forgetting your birthday. I'm such a dick." He threw the pizza crust onto his plate.

"It's fine, it isn't a special birthday or anything."

"All birthdays should be special. Especially yours, you do so much around here and you're always busy with work stuff." He pushed his plate away.

"Is everything all right?" Charlotte asked, thinking today of all days, he should probably have been asking her this.

"It's just work." Sam hated his job. The monotonous days of data configuration were a far cry from where he had planned on going in life. Especially after his dreams of working as a graphic designer at TeleTec were dashed when the company was shut down at the end of his internship. By then, all the big companies had taken on all the staff they needed and he had to settle for taking a job at Computer World. Seven years after his internship ended, he hadn't found anywhere better suited to his qualifications. Or rather, Charlotte thought, he hadn't been looking.

"I'm sorry things are so awful," she knew he was dreading returning to work on Monday. "Why don't you…"

"I don't want to talk about work," he snapped. "It's just somewhere I go for a paycheque, that's all." He grabbed another slice of pizza and took a big bite. A string of melted cheese sat tangled in his beard. "Do you not like your pizza? It's the same we always get."

"Yeah, it's fine. I'm just thinking."

"Thinking what?"

She wondered whether or not to show him the photo, hoping that if she did, it would help motivate him into making some changes.

"I found this photo earlier." She pulled it out of her pocket and slid it across the table. "Look at us, don't we look happy?"

"Yeah, ha, that was a long time ago. Look at my hair. I kept VO5 in business back then, didn't I, with all that gel." He picked up the photo to get a closer look. "I wonder if I still have that necklace."

"Look how thin we were too."

"Hmm." He put the photo back down. "We were younger then. Didn't have to worry about work or paying rent and bills. All that mattered back then was if the pub would run out of Jägermeister, which it usually did if we all turned up on a Friday night."

"I'd love to be that size again." She paused. Almost too scared to speak her next words. "Why don't we go on a diet?"

"A what?" he said with a mouthful of pizza. The string of cheese was now knitted fully into his beard.

"A diet. Try and lose some weight. We could use Hema's wedding as a goal date. There'll be loads of photos being taken of us so we'll feel more confident if we do. What do you think?"

"You think I need to go on a diet?" He sat back in his chair, his face was going red, and Charlotte could see this was not going to plan. "Is that what you want?"

"I think we both could do with it. We could encourage each other, have the odd cheat day together to stay motivated but really focus on ourselves. We could go for a walk every Sunday, just a few miles to begin with. What do you think?"

Their doorbell rang.

"You'd best get that," Sam said. "It'll be for you." He quickly got up and made his way to their bedroom, slamming the door shut behind him.

"Happy birthday!" Hema shouted as she pulled a party popper over Charlotte's head when she opened the door. "Last birthday in your twenties!"

Charlotte laughed as confetti rained down on her as she hugged her friend who she could always rely on for some birthday celebrations.

"Thank you, thank you! Come in!"

They walked down to the kitchen and sat at the table once Charlotte had cleared away what was left of their half-eaten pizza. It wasn't like Sam to leave food like this, so she knew he wasn't happy.

"Have I interrupted your dinner? I'm sorry! Tell Sam he can finish, I don't mind."

"Oh, no he went to bed. Bad migraine."

"He gets them a lot lately, doesn't he?" Hema eyed her friend suspiciously.

Charlotte had to use that excuse a lot for Sam when he wanted to get out of a social event. He never wanted to go anywhere anymore.

"Yeah, he'll be fine. So how was the dress fitting?" She wanted to change the subject quickly.

"Oh, I'll show you photos later, but first, here!" Hema handed over a large yellow gift bag which contained several small, wrapped presents. "Happy birthday!"

"Aw, thank you so much!" Charlotte opened her presents, one by one. There was a gorgeous notebook and matching pen from her favourite stationary shop, a small box of Maltesers, a bottle of Vera Wang perfume, a tote bag with images of books by Jane Austen on the front, and a gift voucher for Waterstones. "These presents are amazing, thank you so much." She hugged her friend and was already planning which books to buy with her voucher.

"You're so welcome. So, how was your day? What did Sam get you?" By her tone, she already knew the answer.

Charlotte wanted to say that she had had a magical day and had been spoiled rotten by her boyfriend. That their walk that morning was romantic, that she'd come home to a gorgeous lunch and that they'd spent the afternoon with their legs locked around each other like they were horny teenagers full of passion.

"Well, you know. It's not a special birthday, is it?" she said after admitting she had been in her room all day reading by herself. "Next year will be something big for my thirtieth, I expect. But I'm not bothered this year."

"Charlotte..." Hema lowered her voice. "If you ever need to talk, you know I'm here. You don't need to pretend with me. I've watched Sam over the years, I was there when you got together.

He's different, lost his drive. His motivation. He promised you the world, and what has he done? You work fifty hours a week, more than you're contracted to do, to keep this place going. You've put aside all your dreams of becoming an author. You never even go on holiday anymore. There's almost no joy in your life. What are you working so bloody hard for?"

Charlotte picked at her nails. "It's hard at the moment. Sam's job is driving him mad."

"Yes, and when you try encouraging him to make some changes, he fobs you off. He doesn't want to listen. Things will never change if he doesn't listen. You're always tiptoeing around Sam to keep him happy." She paused, putting her hands on Charlotte's to stop her picking. "But, Charlotte, are you happy?"

"Things are hard for him right now, in a year or two…"

"Charlotte." Hema gripped Charlotte's hands harder as she spoke. "It was a year ago we had this exact same conversation. The only change is things have got worse. He doesn't want to listen and he doesn't want to change. Back in uni, we were all jealous of you guys as he was the best! Surprising you with weekend trips, cooking romantic meals and God knows you did, and still do, everything and anything to try and make him happy." She paused again to look her friend in the eyes. "Can I be honest?"

"Of course," Charlotte said, although she wasn't sure if she really wanted to hear it.

"I think that…" she almost struggled to get the words out. "I think you're worried that if you leave him, you will be lonely, but don't you feel lonely now?"

Charlotte looked down as her eyes filled with tears. She knew that Hema only had her interests at heart. They'd been through a lot since their first year at university together, from stressful assignments and exams, to dating dramas, and only wanted the best for each other.

"Remember our old saying, 'What would Cher do?'" Hema

asked as Charlotte laughed through the tears, recalling their "Gospel According to Cher". "What is it she said, when her mum told her one day, she should settle down and marry a rich man?" Hema asked.

"She said, *'Mom, I am a rich man.'*" Charlotte wiped away her tears, sitting up straight.

"Exactly. Cher didn't need a man by her side, to support her, keep her going. Be like Cher."

"I just want to make him happy." Charlotte's voice broke as the tears returned.

"I know, hun, but… I want *you* to be happy."

CHAPTER 4

*H*ema's words were weighing on Charlotte's mind that evening and long into the night. Even though her friend wasn't telling her to break up with Sam, it was clear it might be the only solution. She knew that if she were single, and living alone, she would spend her evenings sitting in silence with no one to talk to. She would be doing all her own cooking, cleaning up after herself and going to bed alone, and then she realised, that was how she spent most of her evenings now anyway. That was how she'd spent yet another birthday. Sam was always either playing on his Xbox or glued to his phone, never glancing up to even ask how her day was when she got home from a gruelling ten-hour shift.

Charlotte thought back to the early days when they first moved in together. So many promises were made, *"This is only temporary,"* Sam would say, *"until we buy our dream house, you wait!"* Or if she'd had a particularly tough day at work, *"Get your feet up, I'll sort tea and run you a bath."* Charlotte was always so grateful and would return his generosity in any way she could. Things were always balanced in their relationship. The last couple of years, however, no matter what Charlotte did, no matter how big the gesture, there was no changing the fact that Sam had just lost interest in her, and she couldn't understand why. Maybe he no longer found her attractive, maybe he didn't love her anymore. Or maybe he wasn't brave enough to make the move and break up with her first because he was also afraid of being alone. She couldn't even remember the last time they'd had sex. It was possibly around Christmas and out of duty.

She woke early on the Sunday, but her eyes felt heavy and her head was aching from lack of sleep. Sam was still snoring next to her so she carefully got out of bed hoping not to wake him. In the kitchen, she folded up the previous night's pizza box to go into the recycling bin. The dishwasher had finished, so she emptied it and put the few bits of used cutlery and cups inside it for the next load. From under the sink she took out the kitchen cleaner and cloths and wiped down the worktop, the hob, then scrubbed the sink, as she did every Sunday, and put the kettle on so it would be ready to make a cup of tea.

Quietly, she crept back into the bedroom and grabbed her own laundry hamper which was full with her uniform from the week, her used towels and other bits, enough to fill the washing machine, and set them on to wash. Sam's hamper was also full so he would have to do that once he got up and the machine was free. Saturday's sunshine had clearly been a one-off as the rain battered against the kitchen window, so she would need to hang her things to dry on the clothes horse by the radiator instead of hanging them outside. If only she'd done it yesterday, she thought.

After a cup of tea and a quick bowl of cereal, it was time to clean the bathroom. She did it as quietly as she could as Sam's snores could still be heard from their room, but in no time, the toilet had been fully bleached and scrubbed, the sink and shower were sprayed and wiped and she'd also managed to mop the floor. The bathroom smelled fresh and clean.

"Mornin'." Sam appeared in the doorway of the bathroom. "Can I?" He pointed to the toilet.

"Oh, yes, sorry." Charlotte picked up the mop bucket, quickly emptied it in the bath, and carried it back out to the hallway so Sam could have some privacy.

"Thanks," he said as he closed the bathroom door.

Charlotte checked the time. It was almost 11am so she decided she'd get dressed once she'd had a shower.

Back in the bedroom, she made the bed and opened the curtains. The room needed some fresh air so, despite the wet weather, she opened the window leaving it on the latch so no rainwater could sneak inside.

Charlotte picked up a few items of clothing that Sam had left on the floor and put them on top of his overflowing hamper. She couldn't understand why he hadn't put any of it in the washing machine during the week. It isn't a huge task. On the rare occasion that Charlotte had time off work, she would make sure all her washing, especially her work uniform, was washed, dried and put away so she could enjoy her free time knowing all her jobs were done, like she was doing today. Sam, apparently, did not think the same way.

When Charlotte was finally finished, after clearing a few things in the bedroom, she heard the toilet flush and then Sam making his way to the kitchen. She assumed the bathroom would also need some fresh air now so went in to open the window before her shower.

"Sam!" she called out.

"What?" he shouted from the kitchen.

Charlotte looked down into the toilet bowl. The toilet she had cleaned not half an hour ago was now stained again. This was also a regular occurrence. She decided not to push it as she knew Sam would just shrug it off as a petty complaint, so she pulled the bleach back from the cupboard and, with the toilet brush, gave it a quick scrub. As soon as the apartment was clean, and her clothes were hung up to dry, and she was showered and dressed, she would be able to relax and carry on reading her new L. Rosebud book before Monday rolled back around and her hectic week would start again.

❦

Charlotte put her book down. She was already halfway through it and wanted to try to savour the ending for later in the week. It was getting close to teatime, and Charlotte called to Sam in the living room to ask if he fancied eggs, chips and beans. She was surprised when he said yes, not opting for another takeaway instead, so she put some chips in the oven and when they were nearly ready, began frying some eggs.

Charlotte suddenly heard Sam cursing loudly from the bedroom. She turned off the hob and ran straight to him.

"What's the matter?" she asked.

"My washing, it's not been done."

"I did wonder when you were going to do it."

Sam picked up Charlotte's empty hamper. "Why's yours empty? You could've done mine too."

"There wasn't room in the washer," she said. "I needed to wash my uniform."

"What about my stuff for work? I'm back there tomorrow." He threw her hamper back into the corner of the bedroom.

"Well you've…" Charlotte stopped herself.

"What?"

"You've been off work all week, you had loads of time. I've only had the weekend."

"So I can't have any time off to relax then?" he pushed past her, carrying his wash basket to the kitchen, not wanting to hear any more. He shoved his clothes into the washer and set it going on a fast wash. Sam didn't say another word to Charlotte the rest of the day, or even thank her when she handed him his tea.

⚘

Charlotte spent the rest of her evening thinking over Hema's words to her again. This was not how she wanted to spend the rest of her life. This wasn't a happy life, she was completely on her own in this relationship. It wasn't even a partnership anymore. They were just two people who lived together and barely even communicated with each other. They never went anywhere together, not day trips or even to do the weekly food shop. It was now or never. They needed to talk.

"I'm going to bed." Sam found Charlotte sitting at the kitchen table. "Goodnight."

"Wait." Charlotte checked the time on her phone. Maybe now was as good a time as any. "We need to talk. Can you please sit down so we can chat?" Charlotte didn't want to just break up with him. She wanted to hear his thoughts to see if he would acknowledge that they had troubles and whether he wanted to work on things, make some changes, so they could try and save their relationship.

"What about?" he pulled out a chair and sat down opposite her.

"Well…" She thought for a moment about how to word things. She wanted to approach this carefully. This was a nine-year-old relationship so she knew it had to be treated delicately and with respect. "It's about us."

"What about us?"

As Charlotte was about to speak, as she was about to open up about her feelings, Sam pulled out his phone, swiped it open, and continued with his combat game.

"Sam, I think we need to break up."

LOSE WEIGHT...
...FEEL GREAT!

Do you want to start your weight loss
journey the *right* way?

Delicious Meals!
Tasty Treats!
FUN Exercise!
Guaranteed results

Join Matt Hicks every Tuesday evening to
lose weight the right way. And don't
forget to bring your dancing shoes!

7pm Arrive and weekly weigh-in
7:30pm Zumba with Matt
8pm Wind down and chat

So, what are you waiting for? Contact
Matt on matt.hicks@hickmail.com to book
your place.

CHAPTER 5

TWO MONTHS LATER...

Start weight: 14st 7lbs
Current weight: 13st 6lbs

"Well done, sis!" Matt called out animatedly as Charlotte stepped off the scales. He updated her weight-loss card and handed it back to her. "Another three pounds, that's over a stone since you joined us six weeks ago, well done you!"

Charlotte blushed as the women around her cheered and clapped at her success.

"Thank you."

"All my girls have done fab this week. Everyone's managing to steer clear of those zingy summer cocktails. Even you, Jean." He winked at a curly haired, middle-aged lady at the back of the room. "How was the wine intake at the weekend?"

"None, Matt." She cackled with a toothless grin. "I wa' good. None at all."

"Fab, fab. A small one is all right, don't forget. You are allowed a treat." He stepped away from Charlotte to address the whole room. "I always tell you, if you were to give up *everything* you enjoyed, then you would just pile that weight back on as soon as you got bored of your lettuce buffet and water cocktails. Everything in moderation. Repeat..."

"Everything in moderation," the ladies sang back in unison.

"Yes," Matt continued. "Allow yourselves a treat. Last Friday, my husband took me to a Chinese buffet which was guilt-free because I had compensated elsewhere and went for an extra jog through the week. We can still enjoy what we love. Just balance things out. Right," he looked to the queue of women still waiting to be weighed. "Who's next?"

The last lady was weighed in and celebrated whilst Matt got the music ready for the Zumba class. Everyone got into place and started their stretches to warm up for their thirty-minute dance. Charlotte discovered that she was more coordinated than she'd realised. After just six weeks of altering her diet and doing this regular exercise with her brother for support, her wobbly bits were shrinking, her legs were toning and she wasn't as out of breath as she had been–in her first week. She'd been ashamed when she had to quit after just ten minutes of trying to keep up in week one, worried she would be laughed at, but the support she received gave her the boost she needed to return the following week, and the next, and try again.

At the end of the session, everyone sat down on the floor and allowed Matt to chat whilst they all gathered their breath.

"A great day today, ladies," he began. "I am so proud of each and every one of you. I'm seeing so much progress and I think you all are too." He moved his hair out of his eyes. "We just have one milestone certificate to give out today and I am so thrilled to be giving this one." His eyes welled up. "My little sister has made such amazing progress. I am so proud of you, Charlotte."

Matt walked through the applause and handed Charlotte her

certificate, celebrating her one stone loss. After a further fifteen minutes of chatting to the group, giving them meal ideas, fun ways to exercise at home and a reminder to avoid those fad diet ideas of pills and shakes, he thanked them all for coming and they dispersed.

Jean patted Charlotte on the back on her way out. "Well done, love."

"You can so tell," another woman said. "Especially in the face!"

"You'll hit your target weight in no time if you keep this up!" the last woman in the room said. "See you next week!"

"Thanks everyone," Charlotte said as they all left. She sipped her water and put her certificate into her bag carefully so it wouldn't crease. She would put it on her fridge alongside her half-stone certificate from week three.

Matt tapped her on the back.

"How are you doing anyway? We've not had time to chat properly this last week. Are you all right?" Matt had been very attentive to his sister since Sam had moved out of the flat. He made sure to text her every other day and encouraged her to join his weekly class to help her get her confidence back.

"I'm all right. Getting used to it now, I think. Work keeps me distracted through the week and Hema makes sure my weekends are busy. I have my Tuesdays here. There's always something to do." She smiled.

"If you ever fancy a change of scenery, just give me a call. You can spend the weekend with Dave and me anytime."

"Thanks." She put her coat on and they walked out to the car park together. "Do you fancy coming back to mine for a brew?"

"Oh, I can't." He looked at her apologetically. "Any other night, but Dave's waiting so we can watch the next episode of *The Witcher* together. I tell you, anything to do with Henry Cavill and he's a horny teenager again."

Charlotte laughed as she pulled her keys out of her bag and opened her car door.

"Okay, well if I don't see you before, I'll see you next week."

"Have a good one!"

When Charlotte walked into her flat, she rushed to her workbag which she'd had to drop off quickly before setting off to Matt's class so she wouldn't be late. Her new work uniform had been delivered that morning. She had requested a smaller size the week before after spending a whole week pulling her trousers up.

The weight was dropping from her legs and stomach so she had lost that support to keep her trousers up, which was interesting at a place where she was surrounded by toddlers all day, grabbing at her for attention. Regardless of the inconvenience, she had a sudden burst of confidence that she was returning to her former self. All the hard work was paying off.

She hung the new uniform up in her wardrobe and quickly showered, getting into her pyjamas ready for bed. After making a decaf coffee, she walked down the hallway and stood outside the door to her office. She knew the decorators had finally finished as they had pushed the spare door key through the letter box. She was excited to see her new and improved room, even though she'd not been involved in the design ideas.

"That's what you should do first," Hema had encouraged her emotional friend. *"Get your office set up so you can spend your free time following your passion."*

She closed her eyes and envisaged how the room had looked before.

Old cobwebs covered with dusty insect corpses were plaguing every corner of the ceiling. Heavy storage boxes had left creases in the old, dingy carpet and her desk couldn't be seen under all the piles of papers and boxes. The room had been completely neglected.

Charlotte kept her eyes closed as she opened the door and stepped forward.

Dave, her brother-in-law, had jumped at the chance to redesign the room for her the night Hema suggested a change. Hema had rallied up Matt and Dave for an emergency wine night at the flat just after Sam had moved out, knowing she needed her nearest and dearest close by.

"I'll design it, hun. You won't need to worry about a thing. I'll measure up tonight and get drawing plans up over the next week or two. My guys will have it done in no time. They're quiet this time of year anyway so it won't be a problem."

True to his word, Dave's team only needed three days to complete their work. Charlotte was anticipating what she would be walking into, knowing Dave's extravagant taste and fondness for purple, but there was only one way to see if he really knew what she needed in an office.

She opened her eyes and her vision was immediately impaired by tears.

The walls were a clean white, with dark brown wooden bookcases covering the wall on her left. All of her books had been organised how she liked them, by genre, and there was a special section for her collection of L. Rosebud books.

Opposite the bookcase was her reading chair, which looked like it had been thoroughly cleaned. It had also gained a companion, a matching footstool, so she could sit back and put her feet up whenever she felt like reading and relaxing. On the wall, to the side of her armchair, was a very small shelf which was just big enough for a coaster, on which she placed her coffee down.

She stepped across the new laminate flooring to the window where her old desk now sat, looking out to the fields behind the apartment building. The desk had been sanded down to remove the old cup stains and then varnished. Next to her old computer, which hadn't been used for a couple of years, were new pens,

Post-it notes and notebooks. A whiteboard had been attached to the wall too.

On the windowsill, Charlotte noticed a purple vase, which made her smile as Dave had sneakily left his trademark colour. The artificial daisies were the perfect, final touch to the décor. Her office was better than she could have imagined. There was nothing stopping her now. But first…

She located her copy of *Little Women* on the bookcase and sat down in her armchair, resting her feet on the footstool, and read with a smile on her face until she fell asleep.

CHAPTER 6

"There's a table over here!" Hema steadied the tray carrying her lunch through the crowd and Charlotte followed carefully with hers, mindful not to trip over any of the children running around the dining hall of the Trafford Shopping Centre.

"Remind me why we thought it was a good idea to come on a Saturday." Charlotte placed her tray beside Hema's and put her coat and bag on the back of her chair.

"Believe me!" she shouted over the noise. "It's quieter here than at home with my mum talking non-stop about the wedding. I've come here for the peace and quiet!"

"Is she still driving you mad?"

"I think she's lost the plot." She slid her straw into her Fanta from McDonalds. "We've got my dress for the smaller English ceremony on the Friday at the Town Hall, but she wants me to have two different dresses for the Indian wedding on the Saturday. Two! You know I love my clothes but sorting one wedding dress is enough. Imagine doing an outfit change after the ceremony and before the celebrations, and fitting in a photography session for *both* dresses." She unwrapped her Big

Mac burger and took a bite. "She'd kill me if she saw me eating a beef burger, but," she swallowed, "she's stressing me out."

"You know Mrs Patel will be able to smell beef on you for days." Charlotte sliced into her jacket potato, mixing the tuna with the salad. "She could smell alcohol that time you had a tiny sip of Prosecco."

"Enough of my wedding drama, what's going on with you? Have you heard from Sam at all?" She took another bite of her sinful beef burger.

"No, not at all. He picked up the last of his things when I wasn't in. He just shoved his keys through the letter box." She sighed. "He didn't respond to my last text. Seems like he's fallen off the radar."

One of the first things Charlotte did after Sam moved out was disable her Facebook account. She didn't need to be inundated with other people's happiness and she didn't want the temptation to browse his profile to see what he was up to. So she had no idea where Sam was or what he was doing for the first time in almost a decade.

"Well, that's probably a good thing. You'll move on quicker if you're out of each other's lives."

"Yeah, I guess."

There were a few minutes silence between them as they tucked into their lunch.

"I can't believe," Hema began, "that we're here with all these amazing fast-food outlets and you went for a jacket potato. I mean, I support you so much for getting serious with your diet, you look fabulous but you're going to be walking ten miles around this place at least. You could have a Big Mac and burn it off before we set off for home."

Charlotte laughed, almost losing the food out of her mouth.

"I have to be good, I had too many Maltesers last night whilst reading. I need to be good before my next weigh-in."

"I'm so proud of you, you look so good. You know my mum

will go mad though and insist you get re-measured for your dress."

"Oh." Charlotte had witnessed the wrath of Mrs Patel before, but never experienced it for herself. "Well, if I lose any more weight, I'll just put on a fat suit. She'll be too engrossed in what you're doing and she won't even notice me."

"She has eyes and ears everywhere... Mrs Patel knows everything! But hopefully she won't know about this." She took another bite of her burger.

They both laughed and finished their lunch, tidying away their trays.

"Okay." Hema picked up her bag. "Where do you need to go first? I know you'll want Waterstones, but where else?"

"Erm, nowhere really. I need a new belt though."

"A belt? Why?"

"To wrap around my forehead. What do you think I need it for?"

"No." Hema laughed. "I mean, if it's because your trousers are too big, why not just get new trousers? In fact, why not treat yourself to some new clothes? Your parents sent you some money to treat yourself, didn't they? Why not find some new outfits to match your new, slimmer self?"

"Well..." She hesitated, looking down at her baggy grey T-shirt and jeans which had become a trend she'd been comfortable in for the last couple of years, but now she was losing weight, they looked even baggier. "I guess we could, erm, look at new clothes. I don't know where to look though. I haven't bought anything new in years."

"That's why," Hema linked Charlotte's arm, "you have me. Plus, isn't it your author event soon? Let's find you something fabulous to wear to it."

Four hours later, the likes of Monsoon, New Look, Next and H&M had been truly ransacked as Hema helped her friend find some new clothes she felt comfortable in. She also treated herself to some new, flattering underwear from Boux Avenue. They were off to a slow start as Charlotte struggled to find anything she wanted to try on, but with the support of her best friend, she found her courage and left the shopping centre with several bags of new clothes. Not forgetting a couple of books from Waterstones.

After a cooling Frappuccino from Starbucks, allowing some time for their throbbing feet to recover, they counted all their bags to make sure they had everything and set off on the long slog back to the car. Charlotte thought about all her new outfits, excited to have a clear out of all her old, unflattering and boring clothes, determined to continue on her journey of self-rediscovery.

As soon as Charlotte walked inside her home, saying goodbye to Hema who had to rush home to her mother's demands whilst scoffing Polo mints to hide any traces of her beef burger, Charlotte left her bags of new clothes in the kitchen and grabbed a bin bag, heading straight for her bedroom. She slid open the doors to her wardrobe. Bland blue, grey and black clothes stared back at her. They almost blended into one item. One by one, she pulled them off the hangers, checked they were clean, and stuffed them into the black bag.

Once the bin bag was almost ready to burst, she carefully carried it to the kitchen ready to go into her car to be donated to the charity shop, then she picked up her new purchases and took them to the bedroom.

Within half an hour, the inside of her wardrobe was exploding with colour. Floral dresses, patterned trousers, mixed tops and blouses. There were also some new summer sandals and pumps too. She had something for every occasion, and for the following Saturday's "Meet the Author" event, she had a red tartan pinafore dress which she was so excited to wear.

CHAPTER 7

*C*harlotte was late getting home from work with the Friday rush-hour traffic. Her plan of sneaking out early was thwarted when little Harrison's mum insisted on another "quick chat" which descended, as Charlotte predicted, into an hour-long meeting on making sure the nursery was doing everything possible to suit Harrison's needs.

"No bananas in his afternoon snack," she'd said for the fourth time.

"Like I said, Mrs White, our kitchen staff have all of your requests–"

"And all that water play," she interrupted again. *"He needs an apron, he has delicate skin."*

"All the children wear aprons, they're provided by–"

"I got some specially designed ones, I'll bring one for Harrison. Oh, and I don't like him playing with that George."

"We can't always control who the children..."

"He plays too rough! Last week, Harrison had a graze on his knee!"

"Toddlers always get scrapes and bruises, it can't be helped. Especially when playing on the–"

"Can't you keep him indoors? Keep him safe?"

"Unfortunately, the regulations state that all children must play outside daily because–"

"I just think you could do more for my Harrison, he is a very special little boy."

Charlotte didn't have the heart to tell Mrs White that Harrison's behaviour was so much of a concern that they didn't want to leave him unattended for even a minute. The reason George had pushed him over in the first place was because Harrison had spent the whole day snatching his toys from him. Even toddlers get fed up when pushed enough times.

Nothing had been achieved during that meeting, apart from frustrating Charlotte as she had planned a pamper evening for herself, but now she was stuck in slow moving traffic after her unplanned meeting with Mrs White, and she was tense. Mrs White was one of those parents she dreaded seeing. Unfortunately, as the nursery manager, Charlotte had no escape from the kinds of confrontations from parents who knew best, and it was not the kind of job she could delegate.

As she parked her car, relieved to finally be home, she had a sudden burst of excitement. Like a child excited for Christmas, she was giddy about the author event the following day.

Once she had consumed her home-made tuna pasta bake for tea and followed it up with plain yoghurt with sliced bananas, she washed her hair, shaved her legs and then relaxed in the bath. Leaning her Kindle against her hefty shampoo bottle on top of her white wicker drawers, she turned on Netflix to watch *The Notebook*.

The film was only halfway through when the water became too cold, She should have topped it up with hot water earlier but had been too engrossed in the movie to notice the cooling temperature. So, she climbed out and dried her hair, deciding to finish watching it in bed. But first, she had a very important job to do.

She went into her office and scanned her bookcase to choose one of L. Rosebud's books to take with her to get signed. She pulled out her copy of *Wish Upon Your Heart*, the first one L. Rosebud had released, deciding it would be very fitting to get this one signed as it had kickstarted her love of romance novels and her desire to write her own books. She'd even started writing a book plan when she was still at university but had no idea where it was. It was probably hidden in her parents' loft. It had been so long since she had written and read the plan, she had managed to forget the plot, but it definitely followed the romance theme.

Charlotte opened up the web browser on her phone, clicking onto L. Rosebud's website. There was no profile picture so Charlotte still had no idea what she looked like. Is she tall? Short? Blonde? Brunette? Old? Young? The top post on the page was details for the next day's event. 'Seats reserved for ticket holders only' was in bold at the top of the announcement. She flipped over to her Gmail account and located her ticket, making sure it was downloaded and easily accessible for the event.

Her nerves at meeting her literary hero the next day were making her hungry, so she tucked herself up in bed with some blueberries and put her film back on. Occasionally glancing at the new, red tartan dress she had picked out to wear.

CHAPTER 8

$\mathcal{A}$ warm feeling rose inside Charlotte as she stepped through the doors and into her favourite place. It was like the feeling of walking into your childhood home filled with happy memories. Newly printed books lined the walls. Some were stacked on tables and some had special displays for particular themes. Fresh, crisp batches of untouched pages filled with words yet to be read surrounded her, and the smell was irresistible. She skimmed her hand over the new display by the door, admiring the colourful covers of new releases she would need to buy one day.

"Are you here for the signing?" a member of staff asked, bringing her out of her trance. She didn't recognise him so figured he was new.

"I thought you'd be here," the manager called from the tills before Charlotte could answer. "As soon as I heard this author was coming, I told myself, Charlotte would be the first in line."

"You know me very well." Charlotte laughed. "I'm a bit early so I'm going to have a look around."

"Make yourself at home, love. You know your way around here."

As Charlotte walked towards the sea of books, she heard the manager joking with the new staff member that if he needed any help, and Charlotte was around, to ask her as she knew the stock as much as anyone else employed by Waterstones.

Towards the back of the store Charlotte could see a small podium had been erected with thirty chairs spaced out to face it. A banner stood next to the scene with images of L. Rosebud's books and a small sign to say seats were reserved for ticket holders only.

Charlotte could hardly contain her excitement, but as no one else had arrived as early as she had and taken a seat, she walked around the store, only stopping once she reached the selection of romance books. She didn't want to seem too eager by being the first person to sit down.

Nicolas Sparks, JoJo Moyes and Jill Mansell dominated the shelves as she selected one at a time to look at, although there weren't very many she didn't already own or have on her Amazon wish list.

She suddenly became very aware of a presence, someone stood very close on her right. Moving her eyes down, she observed a pair of very smart black patent shoes with grey tailored trousers sitting atop them. Quite overdressed for a book shop, she thought, until she remembered she was quite formal in her red tartan dress too. What was this guy's problem, she wondered. People don't usually stand this close to people they don't know.

Feeling a little uncomfortable, she placed the Lucy Diamond book back on the shelf and turned to walk away.

"I'm sorry," the man called after her. "Did I disturb you?"

Charlotte turned to face him.

"No, I was just leaving," she lied.

"You seemed really into that book." He smiled, apparently wanting to begin a conversation with her. "You seemed into all of these here, you like romance books then?"

Was he mocking her? Charlotte wasn't sure, but it wouldn't be the first time a man mocked her love of romance novels.

"So, what if I am?"

"Hey," he almost laughed, holding his hands up in defence. "There's nothing wrong with romance books if that's what you like."

"I do like them, as a matter of fact," she said firmly.

"So, you're here to meet this author then?" He nodded towards the chairs which were now slowly starting to fill up.

"Yes. Yes, I am. She's a beautiful writer, no one writes romance like her." At that moment, she spotted some L. Rosebud books on the shelf and was quickly reminded of the plot of each and every one. "She really gets it, knows what women want to read as well as what they want from their significant others." As she stopped herself from fully ranting about books to this stranger, she looked at his face. His green eyes almost looked deep into her soul, his chin dimple seemed to dip as he smiled exposing his perfect teeth. She blushed, thinking how she was sounding like a fool desperate for love to this good-looking man. "So, yes. Romance is, I, well I enjoy romance books," she stuttered. "Especially hers." She gestured towards a sign for the L. Rosebud meeting.

A small man in a cheap suit appeared and whispered something into the man's ear.

"Yes, I'll be right there," he said, not speaking again until it was just him and Charlotte alone. "I have to go. It was nice speaking to you, erm…"

"Charlotte."

"Charlotte. Lovely name. I'm Ross." He held out his hand, which Charlotte shook in return. "I'll see you around."

She turned back to face the books to hide her burning cheeks as Ross left her alone. She was nervous to turn round, wondering if anyone had seen her encounter and witnessed her turn the same shade as her dress. After a moment, she turned slowly and made her way to the chairs, walking carefully as her legs were like jelly. She showed her ticket to an assistant and then chose a seat that was free at the front. She tried to forget about her encounter with the handsome man.

Was he flirting with me? No one's flirted with me for nearly a decade, is that what that was?

Shaking her head, she brushed the thought aside.

He was good looking though, like really good looking. I wonder if he's still here...

It was almost time for L. Rosebud to appear. Mere minutes until she stepped up on the podium and Charlotte would meet her idol. Like a teenage girl eagerly awaiting to meet her favourite boyband singer, she was going to meet her favourite author. The one person who truly understood romance. Someone who knew what she wanted. Who knew the old, sometimes forgotten values of men sweeping women off their feet and carrying them into the sunset.

He really was good looking...

"Okay, everyone. Thank you so much for coming." The store manager was in front of her, speaking into the microphone. All the chairs had been filled and several people were stood around the edges, clearly drawn in by all the excitement. "It gives me such a great pleasure to introduce," Charlotte squirmed in her chair, "the number one, bestselling romance author," she could hardly contain her excitement, a smile plastered on her face, "L. Rosebud!"

Everyone, except Charlotte, stood to clap. Everyone, except her, was cheering. Whistles whooped in her ear, bringing her out of her trance, as L. Rosebud stood at the podium, gesturing to the crowd to sit down. No one else was surprised, except Charlotte, to see that L. Rosebud was a man. No one else was surprised to see that L. Rosebud was, in fact, the very handsome and charming Ross.

Charlotte looked around, looking for a sign that this was a

joke. Ashton Kutcher was going to jump out from the crowd at any moment, filming a new series of *Punk'd* and she was the star attraction. No one was looking at her though. The entirely female audience were now sitting and swooning over the absolutely gorgeous man who was talking into the microphone, hanging on his every word like he was preaching the cure to end world hunger. Everyone was captivated, and once Charlotte turned to face him again, so was she.

"For over ten years you, my devoted readers, have been everything to me. You wonderful people, who have purchased each of my books, have given me the motivation to write again and again. A recent critic," his eyes reached Charlotte's, "told me that no one writes romance like I do, and that one comment warmed my heart."

She tried to look away from him, but she was drawn to him like a magnet being pulled forward no matter how much it resisted.

Ross spoke to the crowd for fifteen minutes. All eyes were on him, begging for one-on-one eye contact. He read a passage from his latest book and then spoke about his next project before he was ushered to the table at the side where his books were piled high for people to purchase to be signed if they hadn't brought their own.

Everyone was quick to jump up from their seats and join the queue, all wanting to be the first to meet him. Charlotte hovered near the back, wondering whether to leave or not. Pulling the book out of her bag, she felt bad that her book was old and worn. It looked like she had bought it from a charity shop, when in fact it was a first edition she'd bought brand new. The spine was creased from the number of times it had been read. That was a good thing, a compliment to the writer, wasn't it?

As she stood at the back of the queue, she couldn't help overhearing several of the women in front of her talking about Ross.

"He's so good looking, isn't he?"

"So much hotter in person."

"Do you think he'll take a photo with me?"

"Don't you think he looks like Tom Hiddleston?"

The queue was going down quickly, no one else was joining it. It was now or never. She had been looking forward to this day for weeks, it would be daft to leave now without even getting the book signed, despite the author not being who she was expecting at all.

As Charlotte's place in the queue got closer and closer to the front, she got more and more nervous. Already embarrassed from their first encounter, she felt like a fool to not realise who he was. How could she call herself a true fan if she didn't realise that L. Rosebud was just a pen name?

Ross said something to the cheap-suit guy standing next to him as Charlotte approached. He walked away when Charlotte reached the desk, leaving her and Ross alone together.

"So, we meet again." He leaned forward, crossing his arms in front of him.

"We do." Charlotte looked down at the book in her hand. "I'm sorry, for how I spoke to you. It was so rude, I didn't realise... I know I should have known, but I didn't and..."

"It's fine, Charlotte." Her insides tingled as he said her name with a smile on his lips. "It was refreshing. Do you want me to sign that?"

"It's, erm..." She held it out. "It looks tatty I know, but I've had it since it was released. I do look after my books, I promise."

"It looks well read." He laughed. "Can't deny that." He examined the book. "This was the first one I wrote. You've been reading them all this time?"

"I have." She tried her best not to morph into a complete fangirl. "I know you will have been hearing this all day, but you're a really good writer. I have all your books."

"Is that so?" He squiggled with his Sharpie inside the cover and handed the book back to her. "Tell me, Charlotte, do you have a–" He was cut off mid-sentence.

"I'm so sorry, Ross," cheap-suit man said. "We need to keep things moving. You have a meeting at four."

"It's fine, Marcus. I'm talking with Charlotte here. In fact, there's a café on one of the upper floors." He looked back to Charlotte. "Could you spare some time to have a drink with me?"

Marcus looked like he was going to have a stroke. He looked down at his watch and then at a clipboard, stuttering in a panic, but Ross ignored him.

"I, erm…" Charlotte really wanted to have a drink with him. Suddenly he was not L. Rosebud, he was Ross. A man. A good-looking man. A good-looking man who wanted to have a drink with her. Thoughts of dating and getting back on the horse raced through her head. She could hear Hema in the back of her mind encouraging her to go for it. She could imagine Dave jumping like a cheerleader at the offer. Her new body confidence was working, she was beginning to feel fabulous again. And here was a man who wanted to have a drink with her. This is what it is all about, isn't it? "If it's not too much trouble. I don't want to keep you from–"

"It's no trouble at all. Marcus can rearrange things, can't you, Marcus?"

"It's just… we need to… we have a car waiting and a meeting, I don't know if we can…"

"Yes, we can. I have faith in you Marcus." He slapped Marcus' back in encouragement and gestured for Charlotte to lead the way to the café on the top floor.

"So, I have to ask," Charlotte stirred her coffee after revealing to Ross her complete surprise that her favourite romance author was a man. "Why do you use a pen name?"

"It was my publisher's idea." Ross leant back in his chair. "They didn't think a woman would want to read this kind of romance if they knew a man had written it."

"That's crazy. You have a talent whether you're a man or woman. Why disguise it?"

"A lot of authors do it for various reasons, you'd be surprised. I'll bet half of your favourite authors aren't using their real names."

"I feel a little robbed then." She laughed. "As well as a fool."

"Don't feel fooled. It's all part of the business." He leaned closer towards her. "I'm glad to have met you. When I saw you looking at the books, I could just see the passion you felt holding one in your hands. You had no idea what was going on around you. The world was blocked out completely. Did you hear the child run past you, screaming?"

"There was a screaming child?"

"Yes." He laughed. "Then the mother ran after him, shouting his name, 'Jayden, Jayden,' she screeched, but you didn't so much as flinch."

"I didn't notice." She laughed too.

"Exactly. You have such a love of books, and the state of this one," he picked up the book he had signed for her, "is another sign of your passion. Have you ever thought about writing yourself?"

"Well, yes." She looked down at her coffee. "I have a plan written and everything, but it's just finding the time. Things have been a little difficult lately." She sipped her drink, not wanting to reveal too much of her recent troubles.

"You should make time. If the idea is there, you're halfway there already." He didn't take his eyes from her, and she could almost feel them.

They both jumped as Ross' phone vibrated on the table.

"I'm sorry, I should take this," he picked up the phone. "Yes, Marcus." He held it to his ear and Charlotte relaxed as his attention was diverted away from her. "Yes, I'm on my way. Calm down, I'm coming." He slipped his phone into his back pocket and they both stood. "I'm sorry, if I don't go now then my assistant is going to have a panic attack. As much as it would be good publicity, I don't like to worry the man too much."

"It's fine, you have things to do," she said, although she was secretly disappointed.

"I want to see you again." He reached to his other pocket and pulled out a business card. "Call me, please. Even if we just talk about books and writing, I'd love to see you again."

Charlotte took the business card and stood stunned in her spot as their hands touched briefly in the exchange. She felt like Elizabeth Bennet when Mr Darcy touched her hand for the first time. Tingles ran through her arm at his touch as she watched him walk away from her.

CHAPTER 9

Start Weight – 14st 7lbs
Current Weight – 13st 0lbs

Charlotte was elated after her lovely, albeit brief, coffee with the charming Ross. She kept the small piece of card with his phone number in her purse and couldn't wait to tell her brother all about him, and the rather awkward way they had met. Charlotte was still feeling slightly mortified that she had had no idea who he was. How could she have been a super fan all these years but never do any research into the actual author?

The day after her coffee with Ross, she had called Matt to have a chat to get his opinion on the whole meeting but he insisted she met up with him and David so they could get all the details in person. Was it a date? Was he just having a chat with a super fan as a gesture of goodwill? What did it all mean? So, once their next weight-loss class was over, David came to meet them and they ventured back to her flat.

"Where are all the biscuits?" Dave asked as he rummaged through all the cupboards. "There must be some hidden away somewhere. You dieters always have a secret stash you munch on whilst watching *Love Island* or *Gogglebox*."

"I keep telling you," Charlotte laughed. "There aren't any. I don't want the temptation."

"Yes, she's been really good." Matt brought over their coffees. "Weight loss champion of the week again, my sister!" They clinked their cups together.

"I can't believe I've lost a stone and a half already. I've only made a few changes."

"They were the right changes though. Cut out the takeaways. Switch your milk for low fat. Reduce your salt intake. Swap the biscuits for fruit–"

"Switch the dead-beat boyfriend for a hunky author."

"Dave!" Matt called out, scolding his husband. "What did we talk about?"

"She knows I'm kidding." David put his arm around his sister-in-law. "But come on now, tell us about the author. Give us all the saucy details."

"There's nothing saucy to tell," she said. "I sent him a message last night, he said he would be back in the area next weekend and he's making plans for us."

"Wait, he's making plans? What did the message say?"

"Well…" She loved her brother-in-law. He was the over-dramatic type who loved some gossip, but over the years they had become very good friends. Charlotte pulled out her phone and read the message. "'Hello Charlotte, so nice to hear from you. Please be available next Saturday at seven-thirty. I will pick you up (please tell me your address) and I will take you out for dinner X'"

"Oh my God, shave your legs. You could be back here after for some rude times."

Charlotte couldn't help but laugh at David's suggestion. She wondered about the possibility though. It had been so long since she had been intimate with anyone. Sex with Sam had been a rare occurrence before he moved out, and his lack of initiating the act did nothing to make her feel attractive or wanted.

"Don't be daft." Big brother to the rescue. "He isn't the sort to do that on a first date. I googled him and he's quite the romantic."

"Can we change the subject please?" Charlotte was not keen on talking about her potential sex life in front of her brother. "What's new with you two? Any baby news?"

Matt took a deep breath before answering her. "The adoption agency have delayed things, again."

"Again? What's happened now?"

Matt filled Charlotte in on their latest struggles to adopt a baby, and how the birth mother had changed her mind halfway through the pregnancy. They understood that this was a possibility, being the third time they had gone through it in their ten years of marriage, but it didn't take away from the heartbreak they felt at each loss. It never got any easier for them.

"I'm so sorry." Charlotte hugged her brother, who couldn't help but show his emotions. "One day, it'll happen one day."

"What's this?"

Dave, unable to listen to the story of their failed adoption again had left the room and returned with a bundle of papers in his hand.

"Hey, put that back!"

"What is it though?" He flicked through the papers. "Are you working on something?"

"It's just…" She thought about how to explain. "It's something I started a long time ago. It's stupid. I asked dad to find it in the loft and post it to me, see if I could work on it, but it's rubbish."

"Pass that here." Matt took hold of the papers and started flicking through them. "This is your plan, isn't it, for the book you wanted to write? I remember reading through it years ago, it's a really good idea. Romance with a bit of comedy. Definitely something you can work on."

"Yes, but it's all jumble and doesn't make any sense. It's all out of date. I was going to bin it."

She grabbed the papers from her brother and rolled them up, not wanting to look at what she had attempted to begin all those years ago.

"Don't you dare bin it. You've always wanted to be an author, even as a child you'd steal Dad's notepads and write your stories in them. He'd always go mad looking for them." He laughed at the memory. "Sam was holding you back. He's not here anymore. What's stopping you?"

She thought for a moment. What *was* stopping her?

CHAPTER 10

"*I*f you lose any more weight, we'll be ordering another uniform for you." Charlotte's assistant nursery manager, Chloe, had just offered her the last Krispy Kreme donut, but she reluctantly declined. Glazed donuts had been her favourite once upon a time, and she would have had more than one.

"They smell so good." Charlotte glanced once again at the shiny, glazed donut staring back at her. "But I can't. I'm saving all my treats for the weekend." Even though the late May weather meant plenty of opportunities to go out for a walk or evening run, she still didn't want to risk it.

"Oh yes. The big date?" Chloe picked up the donut and took a big bite. Icing stuck to her lips and Charlotte's mouth watered as she remembered the sweet taste of sugar. "Where's he taking you?"

"I don't know, he wants to surprise me I guess. Although he did ask me if I had any allergies or dietary requirements, which seemed random." Charlotte was very nervous about her upcoming date, the first date she'd had for a decade, and she was glad to be having a busy week at work to distract her. "I'd best get back down to Apple room to help Amy, I'll see you in a bit."

Apple room was Charlotte's favourite room at the nursery. It was the toddler room, and the most animated. There were twelve children, aged three and four, and they all said and did the funniest things. She thought of them as miniature comedians, offering new jokes daily as part of a stand-up comedy routine. Well, apart from Harrison, who had been causing trouble yet again.

Amy asked her to observe for the morning, as she had heard him shouting a very rude word. A word which should not be coming out the mouth of a four-year-old. Charlotte knew she would have to bring Mrs White in for a meeting about it in case there were issues at home to be concerned about, but she had to witness it for herself first. Especially after the complaint that had been made about them...

She didn't need to wait long. Three minutes after walking into Apple, Harrison shouted it loudly across the room. Then again, and again, and again. It was recommended that they didn't bring attention to a toddler who swore, as a reaction from a grown up meant the action would be repeated. Harrison didn't get this memo, and the more he was ignored, the louder he shouted it.

"Harrison," Charlotte called him over. "Why don't you help me to tidy these shapes up and then you can choose a book for us to read."

Toddlers were easily manipulated at times, and Charlotte's experience meant she knew how to keep Harrison distracted. The shapes were tidied in no time. Harrison was thanked and he ended up choosing two books to be read and they sat together on a bean bag to read them. That awful word was all but forgotten... for fifteen minutes.

Amy gave Charlotte an apologetic look as she knew it meant she had no choice but to bring the dreaded Mrs White in for a meeting. It would make a change from Mrs White calling up to demand a meeting for herself.

Charlotte felt anxious enough making the call to her, but when she arrived for the meeting later that day, Mrs White was not afraid to say what was on her mind.

"Well, he didn't learn that word from me!" Mrs White insisted.

"I'm not suggesting–"

"He must have got it from another child. It's the only possibility."

"No other child here has ever–"

"I never swear. Ever."

"Maybe someone else he comes into contact with–"

"My husband? Are you telling me that it must be my husband?" she snapped.

"No, no." Charlotte feared she was about to wake the beast. "We just need to establish where he might be hearing it so we can–"

"He's learned it from someone here, he must have. My Harrison is a good boy. He would never say that." She stood. "I will be reporting this incident, and your nursery. For all we know, it was your staff that–"

"Now see here." Charlotte stood too. She had put up with Mrs White talking down about her staff for three years, and she couldn't stand for it any longer. "I've never said there was a problem with your child. There have been issues, and I have tried to address them with you so we can work together, but you never want to listen, Mrs White, and that is why we're here today. We've always been here, but you went straight to Ofsted to complain about us." Charlotte had received the official Ofsted letter the week before that the parents of Harrison White had put in a complaint regarding a bruise on his leg and they would need to investigate due to the parents' insistence.

"Well…" Her face turned red. "I was just…"

It was Charlotte's turn to interrupt.

"Ofsted have requested copies of CCTV footage for the dates you gave them. As you know, there are cameras in every room covering every angle. I'm offering you a chance to watch the videos I have compiled together. Something you can request at any time you wish. Would you like to see them?"

"Well, I erm… Yes…"

Charlotte pulled up her tablet and opened the file labelled "Harrison". There were seven videos in total, but there could have been more if Charlotte wanted to truly traumatise Mrs White. She decided seven would be enough to get the message across.

Mrs White watched in horror as clip after clip showed her angelic boy running up to unsuspecting children and knocking them over, running away laughing. He was throwing toys so they would break. Stealing food from other children's plates. In one clip, he punched Amy in the chin. Mrs White was stunned into silence.

Finally.

"Now, as I've told Ofsted, we *want* to work with you. We are not going to kick him out but as I'm sure you can appreciate, we have put up with a lot. He gets most of our attention which takes us away from the other children." She broke off, being careful not to sound too aggressive. "That being said, you do have a *very* gifted child. His numeracy work is fantastic for his age. Better than the other children in his group."

"It is?" her voice was barely audible as she tried to cling to hearing something positive about her child.

"Yes. You should be very proud, but we need to get his behaviour under control now before he gets to school. Are you willing to work with us?"

Mrs White glanced back at the screen, where it was paused on a clip of Harrison shouting his new favourite word with a facial expression which resembled a Viking heading into war.

"Yes," she said as Charlotte reached out and held her hand as tears were making their way down Mrs White's face. "Yes, I am. What can I do?"

Feeling happier that Mrs White was now willing to work with them, and that she had also promised to withdraw her complaint against the nursery, she didn't think her mood could lift any further. That was until she got home and was stopped by her neighbour who handed her a bouquet of bright red roses.

"I took these in for you," she had said. "Very nice!"

Once inside her home, she pulled the card out of the small envelope.

Looking forward to seeing you again on Saturday,
Ross X

CHAPTER 11

*H*ema topped up their glasses with more Prosecco before relaxing back onto Charlotte's sofa. They had just finished their home-made low-fat lasagne and were letting their food settle before raiding Charlotte's wardrobe to prepare an outfit for her date with Ross the next day. Charlotte already had an outfit in mind but wanted a second opinion as well as help with accessorising. She had always struggled to match a necklace to a dress, or pick out a bag to match her shoes.

"Dare I ask how wedding planning is going?" Charlotte asked.

"I wouldn't." Hema let out a long sigh. "Mrs Patel has gone full on mother-of-the-bridezilla with the guest list again." She took a long sip of Prosecco.

"I thought it was finalised after the last argument, haven't all the invitations been sent now?"

"They have. Mark and I had gone over both families and we tried to make it as even as possible. Eighty guests for the ceremony with another fifty coming in the evening, you know, like work friends and such for the reception. But last night…"

"What happened?"

She set down her glass on the table. Both hands were needed

for a very animated re-enactment of the latest battle of the wedding. Hema did a great impression of her mother's Indian accent which seemed to get stronger the angrier she became.

"She calls me up and is immediately shouting at me. Not even in English, she's gone full on Indian rant. Mark had to leave the room, it was scary. She was like *'Oh, why you no invite Sanjay Mistry and his family?'* And I'm like, who's Sanjay? It turns out, are you ready for this? He is the son of the doctor from *her* mother's village who now lives in Manchester. And it would be rude not to invite him."

"So, he's not related?"

"Not even a little bit, but he is connected to the village, so he *has* to come."

"Of course." Charlotte laughed at Mrs Patel's logic.

"She then reels out a whole list of names which adds another two hundred guests to the list."

Charlotte spat out her drink. "Two hundred extra? Where are they going to sit?"

"In their own homes because they are *not* coming to my wedding."

Charlotte had to laugh at Mrs Patel's efforts, because as stubborn as she was, her daughter was an even match. After all, she had learned from the best. She thought back to the engagement party when Mrs Patel almost went into meltdown at the location, which they had intentionally kept a secret, because had she known they had arranged a hotel venue with an open bar, she would have summoned Ravana himself to put a stop to it. They recalled the drama which ensued, when Mrs Patel snuck behind the bar and tried to hide all the bottles of wine and the landlord almost had security remove her from the premises.

"As much as I love my mother, she seems to forget that Mark isn't Indian. Half of our wedding party will be expecting English traditions whilst the other half won't. We can't win no matter what we do. I have made allowances for her but Mark and I have to do things our way. And if that means falling foul of a doctor I have never met, then so be it."

"Isn't Mark actually Catholic?"

"Yes." She downed the last of her drink. "So as far as his grandmother is concerned, the English ceremony on the Friday is the only one we're having."

Charlotte burst out laughing. "Oh no! You guys need to elope, it's just too much drama!"

"Funnily enough, my dad said the exact same thing." She laughed. "Anyway, enough of my wedding dramas, let's hit the wardrobe and find you something fabulous. In fact, I know exactly what you should wear."

Hema was pleased when Charlotte finally agreed to wear the little black dress they had purchased from H&M when they went shopping. She insisted she also wore the thin, black choker they had bought, and used the green River Island satchel instead of her usual black handbag.

"I knew you'd have an occasion to wear it for soon," Hema said admiring the dress on the hanger. "Make sure to send me a selfie of you all done up. You're going to look amazing. But you have no idea where he's taking you?"

"No, none at all." Charlotte hung the dress back in her wardrobe so it was ready. "It's all very mysterious. All I know is we're having a meal out. I asked for a clue on the location, so I knew what I should wear, and I got the impression it's somewhere *nice*, so I think we've made the right outfit choice here."

"Sounds so romantic." Hema sat down on the bed. "Well, he is the king of romance after all. Good thing he's not a horror writer or you might end up at the Amityville Horror house."

Charlotte laughed. "Oh God, could you imagine? Yes, he is definitely the expert on romance."

"Let's just see what he's like in action. What are the sex scenes in the books like?"

"Hema!" Charlotte feigned shock. "There are no adult scenes in his books, he's very proper."

"Ah, that's rubbish. You could have done a comparison. Fiction verses reality."

Charlotte hadn't even contemplated sleeping with anyone new until then. She wouldn't sleep with Ross on the first date, she knew that, but could she face it in the future?

CHAPTER 12

Hair; washed, dried and straightened? Check.
Make up; foundation, mascara, lipstick and eyebrows?
Check.
Dress; washed and ironed? Check.
Charlotte; incredibly nauseous and nervous? Check.

Charlotte was just about ready for the first date she had been on since her university days. Her first date with Sam had been a typical student night in with food from a local, reliable takeaway in his student house with tealights lighting up his desk, which became a makeshift dining table for the occasion away from his rowdy housemates. The food was his treat and he had attempted to make her favourite cocktail at the time, a Woo Woo. It was quite romantic, but what would Ross have in store for them that evening? If he was as romantic as the men in his books then she was in for a special night indeed.

At seven thirty exactly, there was a knock at the door.

Charlotte allowed herself a final glance in the mirror. Her continued weight loss was now evident. She could see it herself in this dress which clung to her hips, showing off a figure she'd not seen for some time. She slipped on her black, patent Mary Jane shoes which had a comfortable kitten heel, grabbed her bag and a small jacket and opened the door.

Ross greeted her at the door, looking positively charming in a fitted, navy suit. He held out his hand to her, which she happily took. "You look beautiful."

"Thank you." She was glad she'd not worn any blusher, for she wouldn't be needing it tonight if there were to be any more compliments directed her way.

She allowed him to guide her down the few steps, worried her nerves would make her stumble in her small heels. They walked towards the parking area, but they were not getting in the limo parked at the other side of the road, were they?

Ross approached the limo and opened the back passenger door for her. "Your chariot, madam." He smiled as Charlotte could no longer contain her surprise.

"I can't believe it." She beamed. "I've never been in a limo before."

"It's quite a drive to where we're headed so I thought we should be comfortable. We can sit in the back and chat before we get there."

Charlotte couldn't believe she was about to have a ride in a limo. She assumed they were only heading into Leeds, which was only a short distance away. She would have happily hopped in an Uber, but this was something else.

Just before she stepped inside the limo, she glanced back and saw several neighbours staring out of their windows, watching their previously frumpy neighbour now looking slender and going out with a very good-looking man who was picking her up in a black limo.

He joined her on the back seat where they sat on an L-shaped cream leather sofa. Opposite them was a small TV screen and built-in DVD player. Two champagne glasses sat in a shallow cup holder, and an ice bucket stood empty next to them. Ross reached to a small fridge hidden inside a cabinet and pulled out of bottle of Moet.

"Can I interest you in a glass?"

"I'd love one," she said as he carefully popped the cork and poured them some champagne. He handed her a glass.

"Here's to a wonderful evening." They gently clinked their glasses together.

Charlotte sipped her champagne, feeling the bubbles tickling her nose, as the limo eased away from her street.

"Can I ask where we're going this evening?"

He turned to face her. "La Royale."

She thought for a moment, wondering where in Leeds this restaurant was. "Oh, not sure I've been there before." She took another sip. "Where in Leeds is it?"

"It's not," he clinked his glass to hers. "It's in Manchester."

After an hour in the most luxurious vehicle she had ever been in, the limo drove down a private driveway and pulled up outside a nineteenth-century, masonic building which was covered in ivy. It drove up to the entrance where a young man approached and opened their door, not making eye contact with either of them.

They had spent the whole journey talking. There hadn't been a single moment of awkward silence as they discussed nearly everything from books they had loved to favourite holiday destinations. Ross stepped out first, buttoning his jacket, and he then held out a hand to assist Charlotte. She stepped out too, quickly taking in her surroundings. The only lights were from the venue in front of them. It must be in the middle of nowhere, she thought. They walked to the door as the limo pulled away, crunching on the gravel road.

A man in a tuxedo opened the large, wooden door, giving them a bow as they entered.

"Thank you," they both said, but he didn't respond, keeping his eyes down at all times. Charlotte wondered why he couldn't respond to them. What kind of place was this? She didn't know, but was fairly certain this wasn't a Wetherspoons.

They walked into a grand reception area. It was wall-to-wall white marble with a red carpet leading them down the centre to where a young woman was stood in front of some gold-plated double doors with a tablet in hand, smiling and waiting to greet them. She was very attractive, not a hair out of place and immaculate skin. This member of staff was allowed to talk it seems.

"Good evening, welcome to La Royale." She had a gentle voice and Charlotte recognised an Eastern European accent. "Can I take your name, please?"

"Rosebud," Ross said.

The young woman clicked something on the tablet and out of nowhere a waiter appeared to escort them to their table.

"Enjoy your evening," she said as Charlotte and Ross were led away.

Through the double doors was another large room, this one filled with tables, and a string quartet was serenading the room full of diners. Candles were lit on every table and even though the ceiling was filled with exquisite chandeliers, the room was not too bright, instead there was a gentle glow on every table.

All the tables wore spaced out so no one would feel overcrowded, or have their conversations drowned out by other diners. The waiter pulled out a chair for Charlotte and she sat down, with Ross sitting opposite her. Charlotte noticed the table nearest to theirs had four old men in tuxes, holding glasses of dark brown liquid and talking. The four much younger women with them drank red wine and were huddled together, giggling and taking selfies.

The waiter walked away before they could thank him, leaving them alone.

"This is quite a place," Charlotte observed, not quite believing she was in there. She was sure these kinds of places had a screening process based on one's finances and investments before they were allowed in. She was used to places like TGI Fridays where the waiting staff practically sit down next to you to take your order, but here, personal space was clearly the order of the day.

"Yes, it is very exclusive. I don't come here often, but I thought this would be a nice place to bring you for a first date; this seemed perfect." He leaned forward, placing his arms on the table. "The food is spectacular, and the rooftop bar is something else. I thought we could have a drink up there afterwards. It's not as pompous up there, I promise. What do you think?"

"I'd love to." She struggled to hide her smile. There was something about Ross that brought it out in her. She seemed to forget about him being L. Rosebud, top-selling number one author of romance. Now, he was just Ross. A very handsome, very charming man who wanted to wine and dine her.

The waiter soon returned with a tray containing two glasses of something sparkling and a single plate with some very small food items which Charlotte didn't recognise.

"Two complementary glasses of Dom Perignon and an amuse-bouche," the waiter said, gently placing them on the table.

"Thank you," Ross said.

"These look lovely." Charlotte was grateful for the small portions. She was not sticking to the diet this evening as such, but she didn't want to be too irresponsible.

"I'm glad they brought these, I had them once before and they're delicious." He picked one up. "They don't serve the same food all the time here."

"Couldn't you just request it from the menu?" It was at that moment that Charlotte realised the waiter had forgotten to leave them any menus to choose their food.

"You don't get a menu here, it's all down to the chef and what he wants to serve, hence my very random request to check if you had any allergies or dietary requirements. They need to know beforehand." Ross leaned forward and lowered his voice. "Yes, it is very pretentious and not somewhere I would visit regularly, but once you see the bar upstairs, you will want to come again. I promise."

They got through six courses of delicious food that Charlotte had never experienced before. Her meals out usually included Nando's or Wetherspoons, neither of which were particularly gourmet. The portions in this place were incredibly small, but they were out of this world and full of flavour. Despite the amount of plates she had consumed, she didn't feel uncomfortably full.

"Shall we head on up for a drink?"

"I'd love to." She placed her napkin on the table as Ross walked around to her chair to pull it out for her. She had never had this kind of treatment before.

Arm in arm, he led the way and they walked down a dimly lit corridor. The deep red walls were illuminated only by candles on tall, golden platforms evenly spaced out, guiding them towards a grey stone staircase which they walked up together. In a matter of moments, they walked through a red curtain and out onto a terrace. The sun had gone down now and white orbs on tables lit up the open area. In the far corner was another string quartet, but instead of classical music like they had as they dined, this band was playing more recent music. Charlotte recognised a very beautiful rendition of *Love Me Like You Do* by Ellie Goulding.

Ross directed Charlotte to an empty table and pulled out the bench for them to sit on, next to each other. There was a heat lamp above their heads already switched on. A waiter appeared as soon as they sat down to take their drinks order and asked if they wanted a blanket. Ross said yes and the waiter disappeared, returning quickly with a selection to choose from. Ross took one and draped it over their knees. "Look up," Ross whispered closely into Charlotte's ear, sending shivers down her spine.

She did as she was told and saw a clear night sky. A black sheet of silk decorated with glistening diamonds.

"Oh wow."

"You will have noticed there are no bright lights out here," he said, still close to her. "They keep the lighting low so we can enjoy and appreciate the night sky like this. Obviously I arranged for all the clouds to disappear for us tonight."

"Ha, of course." She laughed. She loved his sense of humour. It was very similar to her own. "Remind me to get you to pull some meteorological favours during the summer months."

Charlotte was still mesmerised by what she was seeing, unable to pull her eyes away.

"Would you like to dance?" he stood, placing the blanket on the table, and held out a hand for her.

These words pulled her out of her trance. She didn't answer, but stood to join him. Ross held out a hand and they walked together to the centre of the rooftop in front of the band. He put one hand on her waist and pulled her close to face him so they could dance together. She looked into his eyes, their lips just inches apart. It was the most romantic moment of her life. He moved her gently to the music and they were soon joined by several other couples. The heat was radiating from them.

"This place is amazing, thank you so much for bringing me here. I've never been anywhere like it before."

"I'm so glad you like it." His face moved closer to hers. "Has anyone ever taken you dancing before?"

"No," she said, thinking back to when she and Sam would head into town in the early days of their relationship for drinks and dancing at a nightclub. "Not like this anyway."

"I hope you've enjoyed the evening and it wasn't too over the top with romance and soppiness."

"I think it was the right level of soppiness for the first date," she smiled. "I'd expect nothing less from the one and only L. Rosebud."

Ross laughed. "You're really great to talk to, so funny. I don't think I've ever enjoyed talking to anyone as much as I have to you this evening."

Charlotte blushed.

"Would you be interested in going out again?" he asked.

"I would." She leaned in closer too. "I really would."

She allowed her lips to meet his for a very gentle kiss. No tongue, but it was perfect. Charlotte's whole evening was perfect.

Charlotte sipped water in the limo on the ride home. Ross had placed his arm around her and she felt comfortable snuggling into him. Her feet were aching from all the dancing so she slipped her shoes off and allowed her eyes to close for a moment.

"We're here," Ross said gently.

She realised she had slept for most of the journey. Charlotte cringed as she carefully put her shoes back onto her sore feet. The driver opened the door and Ross helped her out of the limo and guided her up the steps to her door.

"I had a wonderful time." He reached for her hand, pulling it up to his lips and placing a kiss on the back of it. "Until next time."

"Until next time," she repeated, unable to hide her smile, or heavy eyes.

"Goodnight, Charlotte. I'll be in touch very soon."

He slowly walked away as she put the key into the lock, looking back at him once more before she closed the door behind her. He blew her a kiss as she giggled and blushed. She wondered if she should have invited him in for a drink, but she realised it was nearly two in the morning, and was glad she hadn't.

The bouquet of roses were thriving on her kitchen window. She pulled the blind down carefully, not wanting to knock them. Kicking her shoes off, she made her way to the living room and collapsed on the sofa. Closing her eyes, she dreamed of dancing with Ross again on the terrace, surrounded by stars.

CHAPTER 13

Start weight: 14st 7lbs
Current weight: 12st 8lbs

*C*harlotte was amazed that after just a couple of months of making a few dietary changes, doing her weekly zumba classes and having more confidence in herself, she had managed to lose so much weight very quickly. When she first had her measurements taken for her bridesmaid dress, she had just wanted to hide in a hole and never come back out. Now, however, she was excited to be wrapped up with a tape measure and have her measurements shouted out from the rooftop. It was the topic of discussion at Hema's parents' house that evening.

"It helps when there's a hunky author after you." Meena, Hema's youngest sister, giggled.

"What author? What hunk?" Mrs Patel lifted Charlotte's arms up so she could measure under her bust. "Silly man, never change for any man. Too many problems, and look! I have to measure you again!" It was the third time her measurements had been taken.

"Mum, she looks great, leave her alone." Hema's other sister, Priya, joined her on the sofa. "I want to hear everything about him. Is it true he took you to Manchester in a limo?"

"No talking about men!" Mrs Patel shouted. "You girls go upstairs, I have work to do. I can't concentrate with your giggles."

The girls giggled their way up the stairs and out of sight when Hema walked in the room with a tray of tea and biscuits for them all.

"Are they coming back down?" she asked, placing the tray on the coffee table. "Should I shout to them that their tea is here?"

"No, silly girls distracting me. I have so much to do and this one," she pointed at Charlotte, "has lost another four inches from her waist in a matter of weeks. There'll be nothing left of her by the wedding."

Charlotte laughed and apologised.

"I'll take the tea up to them later. Doesn't Charlotte look good though, Mama? She's lost two stone."

"Yes, yes, yes, very good. But please, no more, okay? My sewing machine will go on strike."

Mrs Patel took her paper of measurements and disappeared into her sewing room, giving orders for Charlotte to stay put for a few moments more.

"Ignore my mum, come sit down until she gets back," Hema instructed. "Relax for a bit. Tell me, have you got any more plans with Ross yet?"

"He's been busy writing. He texts me regularly though," she said, picking up her tea and sitting next to Hema. She was secretly jealous that Ross could spend his time being a full-time author. "But he's giving himself next weekend off so we're going to go out for a walk to enjoy this summer weather."

"A walk sounds lovely, where will you go?" Hema stirred some sugar into her drink.

"I'm not sure." Charlotte sipped her tea. "He said he'd call this week with a plan. I'll let you know. So, any update on the wedding guest drama?" She lowered her voice so Mrs Patel wouldn't be able to hear.

"Yes and no," Hema whispered back. "It all got a bit heated last night. Even my dad intervened."

"What did he do?" Mr Patel was not nearly as scary as his wife. He was very laid back and loved his daughters. It was not often he involved himself in family drama, choosing to hide behind the safety of a newspaper whenever a debate began.

"Mum was going on and on about this guest list. Who we needed to invite, who needed to sit where, what food everyone should be having, the band, the decorations. I was ready to cancel the whole bloody thing when Dad stepped in and put his foot down... Mum couldn't believe it. He told her to leave us alone. *'Let the kids do their own thing,'* he shouted. And then there was silence. Nothing."

"She didn't argue back?"

"No, not with him anyway. She asked me later on if we could compromise. I told her she could have twenty extras of her choice, twenty! But they're only coming to the evening celebrations on the Saturday, nothing else. It's going to be crowded enough as it is. I don't think Mark knows what he's got himself into."

"He's been to your family weddings before, hasn't he?"

"Yes, but I've always shielded him as much as I can. As the groom, he'll need a holiday before we even get on the honeymoon."

Charlotte had been a guest at many Indian weddings and events, and they were always very beautiful, loud and colourful affairs. Some lasted whole weekends and she had needed to book the Monday off work for her feet to recover from all the dancing, but when Hema started dating Mark, he became her new plus one. Charlotte was still invited to attend, but Sam never wanted to go with her and she never felt right being on her own.

"Have you told Mrs Patel where you're going on your honeymoon yet?"

"Not a chance. She'd have a stroke if she knew we were going to Vegas." They both laughed.

"Okay, Miss Skinny. I'm ready. Hey!" Mrs Patel returned to the room and saw Charlotte relaxing on the sofa with her drink. "I said do not move from the stand. Back on the stand please, you need to try this on."

Charlotte did as she was told, trying her best not to spill her tea on the carpet as she placed it back on the tray, as Mrs Patel approached with the bridesmaid dress which now had pins holding it together.

"Okay, get this on." She carefully placed it over Charlotte's head, minding the pins so they didn't fall out or prick Charlotte. The dress now sat neatly on her body. She could see herself in the full-length mirror and for the first time since the wedding planning began, she no longer feared being a bridesmaid.

The dress cleverly combined both British and Indian cultures. It was a deep green, floor length gown with a floral pattern down one side using gold coloured thread and a sash pulling in around the waist. The neckline was at a respectable height, but the dress was sleeveless. Far too risqué by Mrs Patel's standards but she didn't put up too much of a fight about it.

"Aw, it looks good, Mama." Hema stood. "Really good. You'll have it finished in no time."

"No, I'm not finishing this one until two weeks before the wedding."

"How come? You don't want to rush it."

"I don't trust this one," she said pointing at Charlotte, but this time with a smile. "Every time I see her, more weight gone!"

CHAPTER 14

*C*harlotte burst into her office and found Chloe sitting at her desk. "I'm so sorry I'm late. They seem to have put temporary traffic lights everywhere today. You can tell the school holidays are over and the school run traffic has returned, just to add to the fun."

"It's fine, don't worry." Chloe smiled, standing.

Charlotte was flustered. Unable to find a parking spot near the nursery, she had had to park a few streets away and practically jog to the building. Wearing her jacket in the humid weather had been a mistake. Had it been a few months earlier, even the quick jog would have killed her. She was pleased she could at least manage some exercise thanks to Matt's class.

"Any problems? Any phone calls?" She pulled her jacket off and threw it at her desk chair, picking up a folder to fan herself with. At least she'd had a little bit of extra exercise.

"No problems and just the one phone call. Mrs White rang to say Harrison wouldn't be in the rest of this week."

"The whole week? Is he ill? Are they going on holiday?" Questions were racing through her mind.

"No, she didn't really say much, just that he wouldn't be in. She didn't want to give a reason really and rushed to get off the phone."

Charlotte felt like she had been winded. Mrs White was going to pull him out of nursery after all. Their meeting hadn't gone as she had planned and Mrs White would be going through with the complaint with Ofsted after everything that was said. In all of Charlotte's time at the nursery, even before she became the manager, they had never had a child pulled out. If there were ever any problems, they were always worked out. But for a parent to feel there was no option but to leave made Charlotte feel like a failure.

"I'll call her later this morning," she said, feeling defeated. "See what the problem is. Thanks for opening up this morning, why don't you get down to Apples and let Amy know there's no Harrison this week."

After Chloe closed the door behind her, Charlotte felt as though she could cry. It was true that Harrison had been difficult for them all, but she could see so much potential in him where no one else could.

"Hi, Mrs White, it's Charlotte." Once she had composed herself and cooled down, she phoned Harrison's mum to see if there was anything they could do.

"Hello, Charlotte, thank you for calling back but you really didn't need to."

"Is everything okay? I understand Harrison won't be in this week, is he poorly?"

There was a pause and she heard Mrs White shuffling, closing a door before she spoke.

"I spoke with my husband," she finally said. "We both... we

both realise there is a problem. We have decided to take things into our own hands. We've both taken the week off from work and have him booked to see a specialist for his behaviour to be observed."

"Observed?"

"Yes, I spoke with my brother-in-law who is a doctor. He recommended a colleague of his who should be able to get us some answers. I can't talk right now, we're getting ready to go, but Harrison will be away for the week while we go back and forth for appointments and assessments, maybe longer, but he will be back as soon as possible."

"So, you're not pulling him out?"

"Of course not." She laughed. "Do you think I want to take him away from a place he knows and enjoys, and where the staff are as concerned and caring as you? Absolutely not. Once we know what the problem is, it will make things easier going forward, won't it?"

"It absolutely will." Charlotte could feel herself wanting to cry again, but this time it was with joy. "Best of luck this week, call me anytime you need to, and we'll see you soon."

The phone call ended and Charlotte was relieved that they were not losing Harrison after all. She updated the staff working in Apples and spent the rest of the day moving from room to room, spending time with all the babies and toddlers. Admin could wait.

She picked up her own phone once she was back in her office and saw a message waiting for her from Ross. Seeing his name on the screen made her stomach instantly flutter.

> Hello, I hope you're having a good day 😊 If you're still free this weekend, I thought we could go for our walk around Bolton Abbey. What do you think X?

That sounds like a lovely idea, shall we take a picnic Xx?

You read my mind, I thought I'd prepare one for us. I'll pick you up mid-morning if that's ok? X

That's perfect, I'll see you then Xx

CHAPTER 15

*C*harlotte's week was rounding off quite nicely. There was another nice loss at Tuesday's weight loss group with her brother. Great news for Charlotte, but it wouldn't be celebrated as much by Mrs Patel. Ofsted had called her and confirmed the complaint against the nursery had been withdrawn and they actually commended her for the action which had been taken, which was a lovely boost to her confidence. Ross also promised to call her that evening, and she was looking forward to hearing his voice.

As she had some time to kill, she wandered into her spare room and looked for a new book to read. She had bought quite a few over the last couple of months to keep her evenings occupied but was yet to get through them. Then she noticed her own book plan on her desk.

Charlotte pulled out her desk chair and sat down, pulling the papers in front of her and flicking through them. She had been thinking about it a lot lately, playing the plot of the story in her head like a movie. Knowing exactly what the characters looked like, how they sounded, how they smelled and how they had their own happily ever after.

Some of the detail in the plot definitely needed updating. Her main character's Nokia 3210 may need exchanging for a newer model. Charlotte knew that if a character was going to play a game on their phone, it would likely be Angry Birds or Candy Crush rather than Snake. Apart from a few of these kinds of changes, it was a pretty good plan, she thought.

Charlotte also looked at her computer. The clunky machinery was also very much out of date. Sam had been able to get it using his discount when he was interning at TeleTec. It had obviously not been used as planned and Charlotte didn't think it would even work anymore. IF she was going to get serious about giving writing a try, she would need to invest in a new computer. Maybe even a laptop so she could write in bed or on the sofa. She even thought about taking it to the Starbucks in town after work, spending her evenings there with hot chocolate on demand.

At that moment, she heard her phone buzzing in the living room. She jumped up and out of the spare room, dashing quickly so she wouldn't miss the call.

"Hello?" she answered with a smile. She had completely lost track of time thinking about the potential of her book and planning when she could get busy writing.

"Hello, you," Ross said. "How's it going?"

"It's going really good thanks. I've been busy but that's how I like it." Hearing his voice made the butterflies in her stomach flutter, as though they were excited to be speaking to him again too. "How's the writing going?"

"Very good, it's all getting underway now. I should be finished with the first draft by tomorrow which means I'm definitely free for our weekend plans. Do you still want to go out?"

"I do, I'm quite excited for a picnic. Do you think the rain will hold off?"

"The weather forecast looks to be good, sunny but not humid, so I think we should be all right. We could park up, have our picnic, have a stroll down to see the abbey ruins. Make the most of having a whole day. What do you think?"

"I think that sounds perfect."

It would be perfect. She had not been to Bolton Abbey for years. She remembered begging Sam to take her one summer, but he'd just wanted to stay home, so she had tagged along with Matt and David. Hema and Mark had met them there too, so she'd felt very alone even though she was surrounded by her loved ones.

"Can I ask you a question?" She hesitated, not knowing how to bring up the subject.

"Of course."

"How do you write a book? I mean, one knows *how* to write, but how do you get started on a novel?"

"Oh well, now you're asking. Every author has a different process, or pace. Some plan for months at a time before writing, some plan as they go, and others just write blindly without a plan because it's all in their heads. The end product is always the same. I always start out with a plan all mapped out, but somewhere along the way chaos ensues and I can end up in a completely different direction. Why do you ask?"

"I was wondering, I may have an idea that's all. I wrote down a plan a while ago and I don't know if it's worth pursuing."

"Every plan is worth pursuing. I can take a look if you like?"

Charlotte cringed at the idea of a top-selling author reading her little plan. The thought of it being entertained by any professional writer felt embarrassing.

"Oh no, I wouldn't want to bother you with it. Please, forget I asked. Anyway, it's all handwritten and barely legible."

"Why don't you bring it along this weekend, leave it with me and I can have a look at it for you. Offer some suggestions and tips. I'd love to help out."

She thought for a moment, wondering if she could bear to share this random book idea with him. Would he think it was any good? What if he didn't like it, would he be honest with her if it was rubbish?

"If you think you'll have time to…"

"I'll make time. If this is your dream then I will absolutely help."

Charlotte finally agreed to bring it along, as long as he promised not to read it in front of her and to save it for their next meeting. He would be the only person to have read her idea, word for word, from start to finish.

CHAPTER 16

*D*avid let out a moan as he looked at the table of food before him. He'd left the cooking up to Matt for their evening in with Charlotte. Usually there would be plates full of delicious treats on offer without a care in the world for counting calories, but the table was looking very green.

"Our dinner parties used to be exciting." He reluctantly scooped some salad onto his plate to accompany his grilled chicken fillet. "Now it's all about the low-calorie stuff. It's Friday night and we're having salad. What happened to us? Do we even have any mayonnaise to make this remotely appetising?"

"Yes, in the fridge." Matt laughed. "And this isn't a dinner party, it's a simple night in. Ignore him." He turned back to Charlotte who was sitting across from him and then reached across the table for the bottle of Bucks Fizz and popped it open. He filled each of their glasses, carefully so it didn't spill over. "He had us eating a full chocolate fudge cake at the weekend, and a takeaway last night. I'll be running it off all weekend."

"It all looks delicious." Charlotte scooped some salad onto her own plate and helped herself to some chicken. "So, what's new?

You rushed off after Tuesday's class, and you seemed distracted the whole evening. Is everything okay?"

David returned to the table with the mayonnaise at that point and he and Matt looked at each other, seeming to have a conversation together with their eyes which were slowly welling up. If Charlotte tried, she would have been able to cut the tension with a knife. David placed the mayonnaise down on the table and reached out to hold Matt's hand, nodding for him reveal their news.

"We had some news on Monday," Matt said to his sister. His fingers were almost white from the pressure of squeezing his husband's hands too tightly. He hesitated, before finally saying, "We're having a baby. For definite this time."

David set free his tears which he had been fighting to hold back and Charlotte instantly leapt out of her seat and around the table to hug them both.

She squealed. "This is the best news *ever*! I'm *so* happy, congratulations!"

They all cried as they embraced, tears landing on each other's shoulders, but no one minded as this was the best possible news they could have shared with Charlotte. Once they had composed themselves, they sat back in their seats, using their napkins for a final tear clean up.

"So, tell me, how! When?" Charlotte demanded. "Are you sure it is absolutely definite?"

"Yes." Matt folded his napkin back up. "The mother is due in a few months. Absolutely no way she will back out, or so the agency has assured us, although they didn't give us too many of the details." They had been let down so many times in the past, Charlotte was not sure they could handle another disappointment. "But if all's well, we *should* have our little princess by December."

"It's a girl?"

"Yes, a little girl." Matt teared up again. "We've decided to call her Ivy, after Grandma."

Their grandmother had been the first person who Matt came out to as gay when he was just fifteen. She'd been his rock throughout his adolescence when being accepted for being different was difficult. Her response to his declaration had been, *"Well, that was the worst kept secret in history. Now go get the biscuits."*

"She'd have loved that," Charlotte said, unable to keep her tears back either. "I'm so, so happy for you both."

"The only issue is Mark and Hema's wedding. If Ivy's late we might not make it. Not to mention bringing a tiny baby to a wedding..."

"Don't think about that. If you have to miss the wedding then Hema would understand, you know that."

"Oh, Hema will be fine." David squirted full fat mayonnaise over his very healthy salad. "We know that. It's Mrs Patel who puts the fear in us."

They all laughed and began to eat the meal which Matt had prepared for them, but the conversation remained on their impending bundle of joy.

"Oh my God, we need to throw you guys a baby shower!" Charlotte announced. "You absolutely need one."

"We won't have time for that now," Matt said. "It won't give people enough notice and most people we'd invite are going to Hema's wedding so they have that cost to think about, not to mention Christmas."

"Let me arrange one, please. Whoever can come will come, but we need to celebrate one way or another. And people will *want* to celebrate for you." She looked to David, knowing he could never refuse the idea of a party. He had all the local party suppliers and caterers on speed dial and with the amount of business he brings them they would jump at the chance to return the favour. He loved any excuse to have a social event, especially if it was in their honour.

Matt saw the twinkle in David's eyes and knew there was no point in trying to talk them out of it now. The battle, although very short, had been won. They would be having a baby shower which, now he thought about it, would be very lovely indeed.

"Let's have a toast," he said, picking up his glass of Bucks Fizz.

"To baby Ivy," Charlotte said, which they both repeated. Their glasses clinked as they sipped their orange bubbles. .

"Thinking back to the party," David said. "Do you think it'd be a bit over the top if we–"

"Probably, yes," Charlotte and Matt said in unison.

CHAPTER 17

*I*t was a sunny Saturday afternoon. Ross had picked Charlotte up early and driven a little beyond Bolton Abbey where they could leave his car in the shade of the trees at Barden Bridge. They were lucky to find a space, arriving just as someone was leaving. He had split a picnic between two rucksacks, giving Charlotte the smaller, lighter one to carry, and they walked hand in hand across the fields passing veteran hikers heading off for locations such as Simon's Seat and Stump Cross. Their journey wouldn't be as strenuous, heading just a couple of miles to the small beach near the ruins of the priory to enjoy their picnic in the sunshine.

They walked across the bridge going over the River Wharfe together and past the Cavendish Pavillion which was very busy with families, old and young, enjoying their lunches on the tables and chairs outside the cafe. Most of them had dogs that were eyeing up the ducks relaxing on the grass opposite. As Charlotte and Ross walked through the gate, they carefully navigated their way down the long road, stepping out of the way as cars drove slowly past them searching for places to park.

The couple finally reached the bottom and walked across the

field towards the abbey, standing in all its splendour before them. The sheep, who had been peacefully munching on grass, hurried out of their way as they headed down to a clearing near the beach. Ross pulled a blanket from his backpack and spread it out for them both to sit down on while Charlotte rummaged for the tupperware boxes filled with various treats such as sandwiches, sausage rolls, strawberries and miniature pastries as well as a bottle of orange juice and two cups.

They both faced the abbey as they ate. There was a beautiful backdrop of a clear blue sky behind it with birds flying above. Down on the river bend was a narrow bridge, and in front of it were some stepping stones in the water with people attempting to hop their way across. Charlotte and Ross both laughed as a man lost his balance and fell into the water. As they finished eating, their attention was brought back to the abbey.

"It's beautiful, isn't it? To think what it once was. It's my favourite place to come and think if I find my characters in a plot hole I can't dig them out of."

"I remember one of your books was set around here." She sipped some of her juice, feeling the sun kissing her shoulders.

"Yes, *Love's Lost Kiss*. My third if I remember correctly."

Charlotte knew it was, but she didn't want to come across as a fangirl on their date.

"I brought some strawberries, would you like some?" he asked.

"I would, thank you." A gentle breeze blew over them, giving Charlotte some much needed respite from the summer heat.

Ross grabbed the tupperware box which contained the strawberries and opened the lid. Charlotte reached over for one when he playfully pulled it away from her.

"Now, now," he said. "Where's the romance if I don't feed you at least one strawberry?"

"You don't have to." She looked at all the people sitting around them. Children were splashing in the water, running around near their blanket on the floor. It was not a very private location for romantic gestures such as these.

"Come on, just the one. We can re-enact one of the scenes from the book." Despite her protests, he picked up one of the strawberries and put it in her mouth, tickling her lips with it first before placing it on her tongue. "Are they good?"

"Mmm…" She forgot about the people around them. In that moment, it was just the two of them. "They're really good."

He pulled out another and fed it to her again.

"So how is everything going, how was last night at your brother's?" Ross asked.

They were interrupted as Ross' phone rang.

"I'm so sorry, I thought I'd switched it off." He pulled the phone from his back pocket to see who was interrupting their date. He let out a long sigh. "I'll need to take this, I'll be quick." He swiped up on the screen. "Marcus, what's up?"

Charlotte took this moment of distraction to grab a napkin and wipe the strawberry juice from her lips and discreetly pick at a seed stuck in her teeth. She saw an elderly couple sitting nearby. They exchanged smiles. Charlotte noticed they were holding hands. How lovely, she thought, to be as old as they were and still in love.

"No," Ross said, firmly. "I'm not working this weekend, I told you. I sent it over last night. They'll have to wait until Monday." There was silence as a muffled voice was pleading on the other end of the phone. Ross rubbed his eyes in frustration. "All right, all right. Tell them they'll have it this evening. I'm not at home at the moment but I will be later on."

He hung up the phone without saying goodbye and hid it deep in the bottom of his rucksack.

"Is everything okay?"

"Yes, just the publishers have called Marcus to say they've not received the whole manuscript. There must have been a problem with the email attachment. I don't know why they're in a rush for it, it's a Saturday."

"Do you need to go?" It was already three and would take some time for him to drop Charlotte at home and get back to his own place.

"Soon, there's no rush. I guess we could pack up and slowly walk back. There's usually an ice cream van at Barden Bridge by now, we could have a walk down there first if you fancy it and have an ice cream on the bridge before we set off."

"That sounds good, but please let me buy them." Ross, as chivalrous as he was, had not yet let her treat him to anything. Not even contribute towards paying for fuel or bringing any food for their picnic. She felt like she owed him.

He smiled. "According to L. Rosebud, a lady should never pay. However, an ice cream wouldn't hurt. Did you bring along your book plan for me?" he asked as they packed up the picnic.

"I did," she said, reluctantly. "I've left it in the car."

"Excellent, I'm looking forward to reading it."

"If you *can* read it. It's all handwritten, and from a million years ago. It will be really out of date now. It may not even make sense."

"A plan generally doesn't make sense. Once you get writing it, that's when it falls into place. I'm excited to read it. See what my future competition is."

She laughed as he teased her. He held out his hands and pulled her up beside him and then they both packed everything back into the rucksacks.

"So, is everything all right?" Ross asked. He grabbed hold of her hand as they set off walking across the field. Charlotte hadn't yet told him about Sam. She wondered if it was time they opened up about previous relationships before they really attempted a new one together.

"Look, I should probably be honest with you about something." She allowed her hand to drop from his. "I was in a relationship. A very serious relationship. It only ended in March and we had been together for years. Doing all this is very new for me. I'm enjoying it, but..."

"But you'd like to take things slow?"

Charlotte hesitated. They had walked away from the abbey and were now in the middle of a field, full of sheep, but luckily away from anyone else who could overhear them. Ross stopped and gently pulled Charlotte to face him. "I don't know how I want to take things in general." She said. "I'm really, very new to this. Sam and I got together when I was barely twenty years old. We lived together, made plans. I still don't know where my head's at. I am really enjoying this, but it's still quite fresh, you know?"

"Listen, Charlotte, I do like you a lot. I'm not going to pressure you into anything. If what you need right now is a friend, I'd like to be that for you."

"Are you sure that's enough?"

"More than enough. I've never met anyone like you. Despite what I may write about, I've never really met anyone I want to ride off into the sunset with, as many of my leading couples do," he chuckled. "Let's just do what we're doing. Hang out, go places, and just see what happens."

"Okay," Charlotte smiled. "That would be great."

They continued their walk to Barden Bridge where Charlotte bought their ice creams and they stood together on the bridge, with the sun on their faces, talking about Charlotte's book plan and how excited she was for the delivery of her brand-new Chromebook the following week.

CHAPTER 18

Charlotte was glad to have Harrison back in nursery. It had been very peaceful without him as his time off had been a bit longer than anticipated, but his presence had been missed a lot. It was also time for him to be moved up to the next room, Strawberries. After a quick meeting with Mrs White and a confirmed diagnosis of ADHD they now knew how to move forward to give him the encouragement, education and support he needed whilst not taking too much time away from the other children. Charlotte had received permission from the head office to hire another nursery practitioner who had experience of working with young children with extra needs. She was called Emma and could be there to focus on Harrison to make sure he could thrive whilst in their care. She had started the week before Harrison's return so she could settle in before working solely with him. Mrs White was very pleased with the news, and even seemed less tense when talking with Charlotte from then on.

"Harrison," Charlotte called him over on his first day back. "Would you like to meet Emma?"

He looked at the lady who knelt down so she was at his height when talking to him. She had a friendly face. Her blonde hair was split into two plaits which sat one on each shoulder with rainbows on the bobbles.

"Hello, Harrison," she said softly. "I'm Emma and I'm new here. Do you want to show me around and show me your favourite toys?"

"Yes, yes!" he shouted, beaming with pride at being given such an important task.

"Come on then." She held out her hand. "Why don't you show me where they are?"

He grabbed her hand and pulled her across the room, eloquently describing everything around him. Charlotte knew that this was the beginning of a wonderful friendship.

"Miss! Miss!" Charlotte's trousers were being tugged by identical twin girls in identical outfits, only distinguishable by the different coloured ribbons in their plaited hair.

"Yes, Maisie and Alice?" She smiled, fascinated by how similar they looked, like one was a reflection of the other.

"Can we have a story? Please, please, please!" they chimed together.

"Hmm," she teased. "I normally read you stories on a Friday. It's only Monday but…" Their eyes lit up at the possibility. "Okay then, go and find a book and we can sit on the carpet for a few minutes before I get back to my jobs."

"No, one of your stories," Maisie begged.

"Yes, one of your stories, please!" Alice said.

This day couldn't get any better.

When she arrived home that evening, there was a slip under her door to say her neighbour had taken in a delivery for her. When Charlotte knocked on the neighbour's door, she was handed a cardboard box which contained her brand-new Chromebook. After a lot of research, she knew this would be the best thing to allow her to focus on her writing and kick-start a whole new career. She couldn't wait to get started, and there was one person she was excited to tell.

"It's arrived?" Ross said down the phone. "That's wonderful. There'll be no stopping you now."

"Thanks," she smiled. "I've never had a laptop before. I assume I'll need to download Microsoft so I can get access to Word. Back when I got the PC it was all on a disc."

"It's a lot easier now," he said. "But if you get stuck, I'd be happy to help. I don't mind driving down one evening if you need me. Just give me a call."

"I will, thank you." I was great hearing his voice. Charlotte was pleased that he understood how she was feeling, and that he was still happy to be her friend. After all, Charlotte felt very strongly about him. She was drawn to him in a way she couldn't understand, but she knew it was too soon for anything serious just yet.

CHAPTER 19

Start weight: 14st 7lbs
Current weight: 12st 3lbs

*I*t was five months since she'd joined Matt's weight-loss class and Charlotte still couldn't believe that she had lost over two stone. Her fridge door was now filled with certificates of milestones and she was now joining Matt for the occasional jog around the local park. Her original target weight was to reach twelve stone, and she was confident she could achieve this before Hema's wedding which was still four months away.

"Our weight loss champion once more," Matt began at the cool down session. "Charlotte, my superstar baby sister. She is smashing it, isn't she! It might seem like a small amount to lose in nearly half a year, but slow and steady is the best way to maintain weight loss. You can't sustain a diet if you follow the trends those influencers set out. Just eat healthily, balance those treats, regular exercise, and you can do it! Well done, Charlotte!"

The room erupted into cheers and applause as she was awarded "Weight Loss Champion of the Week" once again. Her fridge was going to need an extension at this rate. The clothes she had bought on her shopping trip with Hema were getting baggy so she had promised herself another shopping spree as soon as she could. She also needed to buy presents for her niece who was due to arrive in a matter of months. Everything was still going ahead. Matt was apprehensive, which of course he would be given their experience and long wait to get to this stage.

David had kept himself busy decorating the baby's bedroom. Charlotte had been to visit and it was perfect. It was a simple cream-coloured room and he had even hand-painted a rainbow which filled one wall. The cot sat in the middle, allowing the rainbow to form a perfect arch above it. He showed her the drawer under the changing table which was filled with nappies, creams, nappy bags, shampoos and body wash for delicate skin. Charlotte had accompanied them to buy all the necessary infant toiletries, using her experience working with babies at the nursery. In the drawer below that were clean white vests on one side and colourful baby grows on the other. All washed ironed and neatly folded ready for their miracle baby.

"That's it for this week everyone." Matt stood. "Thank you once again for coming and welcome to our newcomers. If you have any questions or problems before we next meet, just send me an email. Try avoid texting if you can, every time my phone pings these days I have a mini stroke thinking it's baby news."

Everyone said their goodbyes and Charlotte waited so she could walk out with her brother.

"Good session tonight," she said. "You certainly had a spring in your step. I couldn't tell if we were doing Zumba or ballet at one point."

"Well, you know. Good things are on the horizon. I'm feeling really positive."

"I'm so glad." She smiled. "Do you want a quick brew before you head home?"

"No, I'd best not. I left David unattended with his decorator head on so God only knows what I'm going home to. His focus is Ivy's bedroom but no doubt he will have rearranged the living room and planned an extension if I leave him much longer. How are things with the author?"

"Really good, we've hung out a few times and speak on the phone a lot. He's being really good about taking things slow, but I think I do really like him."

"Well, there is no rush, and as long as he knows it then he sounds perfect. Speaking of rush… I will have to go check on Dave now."

Charlotte laughed and gave her brother a hug goodbye. As she watched him drive home to his husband, eagerly awaiting the phone call to say their baby was on the way, she started to think about her own life. Would she ever be at the point where a baby was in the picture? Could she see herself having a baby? Could she see herself marrying Ross? It was too soon to imagine that kind of future with him, they had only seen each other a few times, but was he what she really wanted?

She began comparing her time with Ross to the first few years she was with Sam. Ross' romantic gestures were like something straight out of one of his books. It hardly even felt real at times. Whereas things with Sam were romantic in a completely different sense. Like the time they had Chinese food delivered to their flat for the first time, but her fried rice was missing. He got straight into his car and drove to the takeaway for it.

Or even the time she had the flu. He made sure he booked the week off work to look after her and as soon as she was feeling better, he took her away for a day in Blackpool so she could enjoy some fresh air and a change of scenery. Those were the kinds of romantic gestures she was used to in a relationship, and Sam knew exactly what to do to keep her happy in the early days, so why did all of that stop? What happened?

CHAPTER 20

9 YEARS EARLIER...

*A*fter finally finishing their last exams to end their second year at university, Charlotte and Hema dressed up in their finest skinny jeans, halter-neck tops and high-heeled boots, and ventured out to their student union bar. The plan was to dance the night away with pitchers of Woo Woo and Piña Coladas in a never-ending supply.

They would be spending the next couple of days packing up their current home to return to their families for the summer before moving into their new flat the coming September, so the night had to be a good one. Their house share had been a nightmare from the moment they moved in, from food mysteriously going missing from the communal fridge to the hot water running out when they wanted a shower. Infestations of ants and mice because someone left a plate of food on the floor which somehow ended up under the couch. They vowed that their final year of study would be spent living in their own two-bedroom apartment away from campus so they could get some peace and quiet, but still be close enough to enjoy the parties.

They each drank their pitchers through long, twirly straws and bopped along to the music playing at this nineties-themed night from the sidelines, observing those around them. There were a lot of third year students celebrating, having finished their education for good, and a lot of first year students celebrating surviving their first year away from home. Hema and Charlotte, along with the other second year students, were just celebrating another night in the student union.

The usual plan on their nights out was to hold off on dancing until they'd had at least two drinks each, but as soon as their all-time favourite song by Cher boomed from the speakers, they grabbed each other's hands and made their way to the dance floor where they loudly and proudly sang every part of "The Shoop Shoop Song", word for word.

They hugged and squeezed each other tightly along with the song, acting out the chorus every time Cher sang that it was in his kiss, not caring about who may have been watching them as they were living their best lives.

"Check him out." Hema nudged Charlotte with her elbow and pointed towards a group of guys at the bar. "The one in the red T-shirt."

Charlotte didn't need Hema to point him out, as she had been admiring him all night, and for the last couple of months if she was honest with herself. She had seen him hanging around the computer rooms whenever she went in there to use the printer. He was always surrounded by beautiful blondes who were all drawn to his noughties boyband look. His dark hair was spiked, with the fringe allowed to hang over his forehead. His arms bulged as he stood with them crossed at the bar as three girls swooned in front of him, which annoyed his friend who was trying to get their attention for himself, but their eyes were fixed solely on this guy.

"He's all right," she said coyly as the song ended and they made their way back to their table. "He's got his pick of the girls already though."

"We can look." Hema giggled. "He's not bad. Wonder where he's been hiding this year."

They supped their drinks, had a couple of shots of Apple Sourz and then made their way back to the dance floor, dancing to the classics from Steps, S Club 7, Backstreet Boys, Spice Girls and Take That before deciding to give their throbbing feet another well-deserved break and sat back down. They opted for a pitcher of water to help them cool down when...

"Is anyone sitting here?"

It was the hot guy and his friend.

"No," Hema piped up, kicking out the two spare chairs tucked into the table. "Please, sit down."

The hot guy sat next to Charlotte, who was suddenly very self-conscious as she could feel trickles of sweat on her forehead from all the dancing.

"I'm Sam," he said.

"Charlotte." She wanted to play it cool, but her cheeks were burning. His smile had the potential to melt her to her chair.

"I'm Ben," the other guy said, animatedly. "Do you want to dance?" he asked Hema.

"Sure!" She hopped up from her chair as if forgetting her already aching feet, and they danced their way to the dance floor, leaving Charlotte and Sam alone.

"I've seen you around campus," he said, taking her by surprise.

"You have?"

"Yes, usually with your head in a book while walking around corridors."

She laughed. Hema was always saving her life by pulling her out of the way of closed doors or oncoming traffic when she was lost in a world of literature and not paying attention to the real world around her.

"Oh, yes, what can I say? I love reading." She brushed her fringe away from her sticky forehead. "Do you like books?"

"Not so much." He leaned forward on the table. "I've read a

few graphic novels, but it's computers for me. I'm studying computer engineering."

"Ah, a Bill Gates wannabe then?" Charlotte teased.

"Ha-ha, not quite but you never know where things might lead. Are you in the Creative Writing class then?"

"No, English Literature, but I did study a writing module last year. I *would* love to be a writer one day and have my books out there in book shops. That's the dream. I actually starting writing a–"

Their table jolted as they were joined by the three drunk blonde girls who had been crowded around Sam when he was stood at the bar. Charlotte looked around and saw Hema and Ben practically eating each other's faces in the middle of the dance floor as Vanilla Ice serenaded them in the least romantic way ever.

"Sam," one of the girls said. "Let's get some more shots," she slurred.

"Yeah, come on, it's your turn." The taller of the three leaned across the table in the direction of Sam, pushing out her cleavage so much it almost popped out of her tiny top. "We got the last round."

Charlotte felt awkward as the third girl went one step further and walked behind Sam, putting her hands on his shoulders and rubbing them down his chest. She was about to get up and leave, seeing he had all the female company he needed, when she saw him shrug away the girl's touch.

"Girls, come on," he growled. "Not now, yeah?"

Charlotte smiled to herself as the girls finally took the hint and left them alone, shooting her a look that could kill.

"Sorry about that," he said. "They've been following us around all night. I felt like I needed some kind of fly spray or fireman's hose to get rid of them."

"They're very pretty," Charlotte said.

"So are tigers, but you wouldn't want them crowding you

either. They're not my type."

"What is your type?" She sipped her water.

Sam smiled at her again and Charlotte felt goosebumps tingle their way down her spine just as Ricky Martin started singing "Livin' La Vida Loca" through the speakers.

"Do you want to dance?"

"Erm…" Charlotte blushed again. "I would but I feel so gross now from dancing all night."

"Well, I think you look nice. And the night's almost over, I'd hate to miss out on at least one dance with you."

He stood, holding out his hand which Charlotte took hold of as he led her to the dance floor. They danced to Ricky Martin, Christina Aguilera and Sir Mix-a-Lot. At some point, she glanced over to see Hema and Ben getting even closer, if possible, and making their way out of the door into the night. Charlotte realised she would have to make her own way home. Sam spied his friend leaving too.

"Do you want me to walk you home?" he asked.

"You don't have to, it's not far from here." She didn't want him to go out of his way for her.

"No, please, I insist. I won't be able to sleep if I let you walk home on your own."

Charlotte couldn't believe that the hottest guy on campus wanted to walk her home. The fact that the three blonde girls were still glaring at her was an added bonus. At that moment, the lights in the bar switched on, triggering the end of the night. It was after midnight and so time to go home. Everyone around them was sweaty from all the dancing, which is unavoidable when it's a themed pop night like this. They were always popular.

"Did you bring a coat?" Sam asked.

"No." She linked onto Sam's arm when he held it out for her. As she stood close to him, she could smell his Calvin Klein aftershave, and she led him in the direction of her house.

They talked all the way there and discovered they were from

the same hometown. The more they talked and got to know each other, the more smitten Charlotte became. They laughed together, discovered they were both just finishing their second year and would be living very near to each other from September. They loved the same movies, same music and food. It was all very perfect.

"Can I get your number?" he asked as they got to her door.

She typed it into his phone and he slipped it back into his pocket. He bid her goodnight by kissing her on the cheek and then walked away with a promise of calling her the next day to arrange a romantic first date.

CHAPTER 21

*T*here was a chill in the air, which was typical for late British summer weather. Charlotte was still sporting a tan from her trip to Bolton Abbey with Ross just a couple of weeks before. Ross had suggested they keep their next date simple, so he picked her up in his BMW and drove them into Ilkley. The recently trimmed grass crunched under their feet as they walked along the river before enjoying an afternoon tea at Betty's Café Tea Room. She had only been there once before.

The original plan had been for Sam to take her after her mum had sent vouchers for her birthday a few years ago, but he had pulled out at the last minute not wanting to trek into Ilkley on a weekend when it would be busy with families and young children, so Hema went in his place. They had giggled over how small the sandwiches were, comparing the experience to a food tasting session, and these were in fact samples of what they could have if they liked them. Charlotte knew Sam wouldn't have enjoyed it as much as they did.

"I read your book plan." He poured their coffees as Charlotte felt her stomach wobble at the mention of her measly plan for a book.

"You really didn't need to. You're busy with your own book stuff. You don't need to spend any time on mine."

"I have plenty of time, I'm just waiting for them to return the edited version to me at the moment anyway so it's perfect timing. Honestly though, Charlotte..." He put down the cafetière and placed his hands on hers on the table. "It is absolutely fantastic."

"It... is it?"

"Yes." He poured a dash of milk into his coffee. "Your take on contemporary romance is fresh, it's new, and there's an element of comedy in there too. It is something the market definitely needs right now. Do you think you could give the first few chapters a go? You have your new laptop all set up now, don't you?"

"You mean, sit and actually write it?" It was one thing creating a plan, imagining her characters and what they might look like, dress like, smell like. If they might strut down a street or saunter. If they are witty or serious. Handsome or beautiful. But how would she convert the images in her mind into actual words?

"Yes, here." He reached into his bag and pulled out the papers. "I made a couple of notes in red, but they're just suggestions based on my opinion only. Don't take it as gospel, but please, give it a go. I'd love to offer any help I can."

"Okay, I think I will." She was elated, but also nervous. She had studied her plan before giving it to him, and now knew the story idea like the back of her hand. She had no problems making up stories to tell the children at nursery, but this one was different. And even if she did manage to write it, how on earth would she get it published?

"Great. Oh, these jam tarts are to die for." He pulled one from one of the tiers of the cake stand and put it on her plate. "Just take a bite, it's divine."

The tart was in fact delicious, he had been right about that. Charlotte had intentionally been careful with her diet during the week so she could indulge on some baked treats with Ross at the weekend.

"How long until you get the manuscript back, do you think?" Charlotte asked.

"They haven't said. It usually takes a month or two for the first reads to be done. Then they'll send it back for me to give a final proofread, it's probably looking at a summer release next year, if not sooner."

"I'll be sure to get it pre-ordered then." She wondered if he would share some of the plot with her now, but decided not to ask, not wanting to take liberties as a close friend of the author.

"No need." Ross reached into his bag and pulled out some papers bound in a black, plastic cover. "I have it here for you. An exclusive."

"Oh my God, are you serious?" Charlotte quickly wiped her hands on her napkin before taking the manuscript from him, not wanting to make it sticky from jam and cream.

"You're going to be the first person to read it. I can't wait to see what you think."

Charlotte noticed Ross' eyes as he handed over his latest project. She glanced at his lips before quickly looking away, not sure if that was an urge to kiss him or not.

Their afternoon tea, although small portions of sandwiches, cakes and scones, was very filling. They finished the last of the coffee and Ross paid, again, despite Charlotte's insistence of paying, and they headed out together.

"I can't believe it's September already. Are you free the rest of the day?" he asked. "We could go for a walk along the river."

"Actually no, I'm helping to plan a baby shower for my brother next weekend and I have some things on my list." Charlotte had almost forgotten about her job for that afternoon.

She had written a list in her phone. David was in charge of decorations, of course, but she insisted on taking charge with the food.

"That sounds nice, I remember you saying they'd been trying to adopt."

"Yes, it's been a long process. They're ready to be parents now though, and they're going to be brilliant dads, I can tell." She smiled.

"Do you want children, one day?"

"Erm, well…" It was the age-old question that single women get asked when they are about to hit thirty. A question where no answer was ever really the whole truth, because when you are single and on a date with someone you haven't known for that long, what is the right answer? What if she didn't want children, but changed her mind in a few years, was that allowed? "It's always something I've wondered about, but I'm not pressuring myself. You?" If Charlotte had to answer this question, then so did he.

"It would be very lovely. With the right woman, it would be very lovely indeed."

They walked back to the car alongside each other, hands only inches apart. Charlotte fought against her urge to grab his hand. To let him hold hers tightly. To let herself completely go and be available for him.

CHAPTER 22

*H*ema called Charlotte the following Wednesday evening just as she was about to settle with a hot chocolate and watch some trash, midweek television. "Hey, can I come over?"

"Of course, is everything all right?"

"Yes, fine." Hema sounded stressed. "Mark's away for work and my mum is calling me every five bloody minutes with questions about the wedding. I need a break."

"Come over." She laughed. "I'll put the kettle on."

"You're a lifesaver, see you soon."

Charlotte found her emergency stash of chocolate digestive biscuits for the occasion, that she had cleverly hidden so even David couldn't find them. She'd sensed they would be needed at some point, and just fifteen minutes after her call, Hema was knocking on the door. She walked in with her phone attached to her ear and talking at full speed, barely stopping to take a breath.

"Mama, no, Mama, what did I say? What did I say? I don't

want any of that... I don't care... then you have one for yourself, I'm not coming. What? Mama, I have to go – I'm at Charlotte's now. Yes, I am. Yes, I'll tell her. I'll tell her, Mum!" She exhaled loudly and looked at Charlotte, tilting her phone towards her. "Mum says it's your final dress fitting on 12th December. Don't forget. Don't be late. Don't lose any more weight!"

"Okay, Mrs Patel!" she called out for her to hear, although she couldn't make any promises about the weight which was still successfully dropping off her. The kettle had just boiled so she poured their drinks out whilst Hema continued her battle on the phone.

"There, Mama, I told her. No, I wasn't mocking your accent. I have to go. I have to go, Mama... Mama... Mum! Yes, I'll see you at the weekend. Goodbye." She clicked off the call. "Argh!"

"Biscuit?" Charlotte held out the packet and Hema took a handful.

"This wedding's going to kill me."

"Clearly weddings are the happiest of times." She pulled a biscuit from the packet and took a small bite, planning to savour every crumb and taste.

"I was talking to my cousin Ameera last night, she got married in London last year." Hema took a bite of a biscuit and it crunched as she spoke. "Apparently, her mother had a stroke the week before the wedding because of the stress of it all."

"A stroke? Oh my God, is it really all worth giving yourself a stroke?"

"My mum didn't appreciate me reminding her of it earlier. She's *impossible*. I mean, I do love the Indian traditions, and Mark's happy to embrace them, but for our wedding I want it to be about us coming together. I don't want to do things because I *have* to. Our children will be half of me and half of him but my mum seems to think they'll be raised the way I was."

"You're an adult and you're allowed to dictate your life the way you want." She picked up their drinks whilst Hema clung to the biscuits and they made their way to the living room to collapse on the couch. "Don't be forced into anything. Anyway, when did having children go on the menu? I thought you guys weren't going to bother?"

They'd had this discussion not long after Hema started dating Mark. Hema had not wanted children, wanting instead to focus on her photography career which involved a lot of travel around the country, and Mark was not fussed either way. He would have been happy if they did have kids as much as he would if they didn't.

"We've been talking about it a lot, since hearing Matt and David's news. David sent me some photos of the baby's room and it looks adorable. So, we figured, maybe after a year or two, we might start trying. After all, we'll be thirty next year so if we don't do it now then what's the point of..." she stopped herself. "I mean, well, you know what I mean."

"It's all right, thirty isn't old. We still have plenty of time."

"So how are things going with the author?" She picked up her coffee. "Do you see it potentially becoming anything?"

Charlotte finished her biscuit and allowed herself to have another. "He's lovely and good-looking. Very attentive, romantic, says all the right things, is very interested in me and what I'm doing. He is very supportive of me pursuing a career in writing. All of these being things I am not used to."

"Aw, he sounds so perfect!" Hema beamed.

"Yes," she hesitated. "It all sounds perfect on paper, doesn't it?"

"And isn't it?"

Charlotte thought before she spoke, wondering herself if she could see things going any further with Ross.

"I don't know. Sam was all of those things in the beginning. He was thoughtful and caring. Wanted me to pursue a career in writing. And then it all just went..." she sighed, not able to finish. "What if it doesn't go anywhere with him or anyone ever again?

Am I going to be the spinster aunt to baby Ivy and your potential, future children?"

"Look, you were with Sam from such a young age, and for such a long time, don't be so hard on yourself. All of his habits are still imprinted in your mind, you could end up with Ross or date another ten guys and you will still compare them all to Sam. It's only natural, but don't force it with Ross if it's not there. When are you seeing him again?"

"There aren't any plans yet, he knows I'm busy this weekend so we'll probably talk next week and arrange something. I just wish I could be in control. He takes me to some amazing places, and I do have a good time, but I want to make the decisions for once. Show him that it's not just down to the guy to do all the legwork, do you know what I mean? I'd love to treat him to something special."

"Why don't you invite him here?"

"Here?" She looked around at her tiny flat, wondering what he would make of it. She loved her flat, it was a perfect size for her living on her own, but it needed sprucing up. She thought about asking David to help her out, modernise it a bit.

"Yes, invite him here. It's your territory, you'll be in control. Maybe then you'll know how you feel about him on your own turf."

Charlotte wondered, and it was not a bad idea at all.

CHAPTER 23

7 YEARS EARLIER

Sam's Ford Fiesta cruised north along the A1 motorway. They had just left the service station after enjoying the obligatory pre-holiday Burger King which, ordinarily, would have been enjoyed at Manchester Airport. However, their lack of funds meant this summer holiday would instead be a day trip somewhere new. Sam wanted to make it as special for Charlotte as possible so had kept the location secret.

The typical August weather threatened rain and storms in the distance as they drove along, with Charlotte trying to guess where they were headed from the road signs. Her geographical skills weren't great, but she had picked up that they were travelling north.

"Durham?" she asked, knowing it was famous for its cathedral, but they were not heading to Durham. "Newcastle?" she asked as they drove past the Angel of the North, but they were not going to Newcastle. "Where are we going?"

"It's a surprise." He took one hand off the wheel and gripped her leg. "I promise you, you'll love it."

Charlotte thought about how amazing her boyfriend was. He had just completed his first year at TeleTec, a very low-paid internship for very long hours, and in just a few days he would find out what his permanent position would be within the company. He was hoping for the Junior Executive role which had a great beginner's salary that would increase year after year, as well as bonuses, a company car and insurance all paid for. This would free up some outgoings so Charlotte could leave her part-time job at the nursery as a childcare assistant and write books in the office which Sam had set up for her in their new flat. Everything was falling into place for them, just as they had planned.

They exited the motorway and signs for Alnwick appeared. The castle created an enchanted backdrop amongst the greenery and quiet, winding roads. Was the castle their destination? She had not been since she was a little girl, but always remembered the grand rooms and staircases and, more importantly, the collection of antique books she was always hungry to get her fingers on.

"Not the castle," Sam quipped. "We might not have time. It depends…" he teased. "But we're almost there."

Charlotte racked her brains. Somewhere in Alnwick that she would love, but not the castle. Where was he taking her?

"Barter Books!" she squealed. "Oh my God, are you serious?"

She had forgotten all about this bookshop. She had read about it the year before, reading out the reviews from Google to him as they lay in bed together one Sunday morning. *"A magical experience – a book lover's dream – already planned a return trip!"*

They left their car in a small car park nearby and walked hand in hand to the bottom of the path where "Barter Books" in golden letters created a welcoming archway above them, inviting them to step forwards into a world of literary wonder. Trees lined the path, and the leaves were already showing signs of an orange tint.

"I can't believe I'm here," she gushed. "What made you think of here of all places?"

"You talked about it so much, how could I not bring you?

Anyway, I wanted to surprise you and the gruelling nightmare that is the A1 was absolutely worth it to see your face just now."

She was still grinning as Sam held open the door and they stepped inside.

"Is this it?" he whispered in her ear. "I thought there'd be more to it than this."

Charlotte shared his disappointment as the few racks of second-hand books surrounded them, with a log fire in the corner with a few comfy chairs in front of it. There wasn't a lot to take in. It appeared to be just a regular bookshop.

"Well," she said, not wanting to put a downer on their trip after driving all this way. "There might be some book treasures hidden among these, let's have a look."

Charlotte walked down towards the fire which was crackling as the traditional British August weather meant there was a chill in the air outside, with a threat of rain looming in the distance. A middle-aged woman wearing a tartan shawl sat reading a book with a Shih Tzu snuggled on her feet. Charlotte turned to face the window, bitterly disappointed that the place she had been dreaming about for so long was just another mediocre, second-hand bookshop. She couldn't understand how the reviews could have said that...

"Oh... My... God."

"What?" Sam rushed up to her. She had turned round, her back now faced the window and she pointed to the space in front of her. Sam turned and the sight even took his breath away.

Books.

Rows upon rows of books stretched as far as the eye could see. There was so much to take in before them, it took a few moments for their eyes to adjust.

"You may lose me in here, just so you know."

They held hands as they stepped forwards together into the main shop and looked in astonishment at the world of books they had walked into. There was something for everyone:

thrillers, horrors, paranormal, romance, history, science fiction, crafts, sport, diet. There was also an entire section dedicated to antique books protected by screens of glass. Absolutely every kind of book you could imagine, and Charlotte knew she would need an entire day to make her way around it all. Charlotte felt like Belle when the Beast finally showed her his hidden library for the first time.

"I tell you what," Sam looked at his watch. "Let's reconvene in an hour for a coffee, then resume the mad book shop. Deal?"

"Deal." They quickly kissed and departed. Charlotte made her way to the romance section whilst Sam found the science fiction books.

Charlotte smiled, still not believing where she was, and wondered how Sam had managed to keep this secret from her. He was truly the most thoughtful, romantic boyfriend anyone could ever have for thinking of bringing her to her idea of paradise.

CHAPTER 24

Charlotte helped Matt to pin the faux ivy backdrop to the wall of their conservatory whilst David pinned pink, fake flower heads around it. They had spent the whole morning getting the house ready for their guests to celebrate the upcoming arrival of their precious little Ivy. Everything was going smoothly, and even Matt seemed to relax, accepting that nothing was going to go wrong this time. Their baby was really on the way, and it was time to get ready.

There was a garland of balloons in different shades of pink forming an archway into the conservatory where the food would be served. A caterer had delivered trays of all kinds of sandwiches, quiches and finger foods. The local bakery had delivered a selection of brownies and muffins and Charlotte had ordered one of their specialty cakes as a surprise. David had done the finishing touches to Ivy's bedroom, excited to let their guests see it, and Charlotte made sure everything was ready in time for their guests.

"Mum called from the motorway," Matt said as they fluffed the couch cushions. "They're going to be a little bit late but said not to worry."

"Oh right, did they say why?" Charlotte asked.

"They just want to check into their hotel first and freshen up. You know what they're like. They'll get here when they get here, they said not to wait for them."

"Fair enough." She did the finishing touches to the decorations and stepped back to look at their work. "Well, big bro, I think we're ready to party."

"I think we are." He looked around the room, taking it all in. "You know David will have a stroke when the baby is crawling and leaving finger marks all over the white walls."

They both laughed as David entered the room.

"What's funny?" he asked.

"Nothing, love. Nothing." Matt stood with his hands on his hips. "What do you think? I think we're ready."

"It's beautiful." He beamed, looking quite flustered. "And our first guests are here. I can't believe how many people RSVP'd. Do you think we have enough food? Is there enough to drink?" He picked up a napkin to fan himself. "Quick, open a window, get the music on, I'll get the door."

"Alexa, play *Baby Shower Playlist*." Matt opened the window to allow some cool air into the room. "He'll calm down once he's had a glass of Prosecco."

Alexa started to play Justin Bieber's "Baby" as the first lot of guests arrived.

It was Charlotte's job to arrange all the presents on the coffee table, ready to be opened after games and food. She needed to leave some on the floor as there were more than they had expected. Hema and Mark arrived with a hamper of goodies ranging from baby wipes and creams to vests, socks and seasonal winter attire such as hats, mittens and thick woolly cardigans.

She had also included several board and cloth books, including one called *My Daddies and Me*.

Charlotte pulled her phone out of her pocket to check the time and saw there was a message from Ross.

Hope all goes well today. Thinking of you Xx

Sweet and attentive, she thought, wondering if she should have invited him to introduce him to everyone. Charlotte knew her brother wouldn't have minded. However, she had been very busy helping the guys out with the party, getting there early to pick Matt up so they could drive around to pick up certain things. It wouldn't have been fair on Ross if he'd been there. Putting her phone away she decided to reply later on. He would understand that she was busy.

"How's it all going, do you need a hand?" Mark found Charlotte in the lounge, walking in just as some of the presents toppled over.

"Oh, please," she said. "I can't get some of these to stand up properly, I don't think they were expecting so many."

Mark walked around the other side of the table and helped to pick them up and rearrange them.

"At your wedding, can I make a request?" she asked.

"Of course, what's up?"

"Please don't put me in charge of presents." They both laughed. "It's far more stressful than it should be."

"Ha, I won't. I'm sure Mrs Patel will have it all under control anyway." Charlotte agreed and they finally had all the presents arranged. "So, listen," he said. "I don't know if you want to hear this, Hema wasn't sure either but, I bumped into Sam yesterday."

"Oh?" she was lost for words, not sure what to do with herself. Two of the presents she had carefully balanced toppled back to the floor. "And, erm, is he all right?" Charlotte still hadn't been back onto social media since the breakup, so had no chance to look him up and see what he had been doing.

"He seemed different, we had a good chat and–"

"Come on then, missy!" A giddy David practically bounced into the room. "Let's get this party started. I've lined everyone up to 'pin the dummy on the baby' but I can't find the blindfold."

"I know where it is." She stood. "I'm coming." She went to follow David out but turned back to Mark. "I hope he's okay, I really do, but I don't think I'm ready to know much more about him just yet."

"I understand, like I said, we weren't sure. But if I didn't say anything it would just play on my mind, but he did ask a favour of me."

"Oh?"

"He has wanted to call you, pop by for a visit to talk about things, but he wasn't sure how you'd feel about that. To be honest, he seemed a bit anxious just talking to me. He asked me if I could ask you to call him."

Charlotte didn't know how to respond, or what she *wanted* to respond.

"Thanks, I'll think about it."

"That's all he wanted. I won't say any more."

She smiled and then turned to find her brother-in-law.

Charlotte let herself sink into the couch, placing her feet on the empty coffee table, surrounded by unwrapped gifts. Her eyes felt heavy after a very busy day.

"We have been well and truly spoiled," Matt said to David. "I'm glad we didn't go mad buying things ourselves. Ivy has enough clothes to see her through her first year of life."

David chuckled. "She now has more clothes than I do, and that's saying something. I can't believe how much your mum and dad brought us. That was really nice of them. No wonder they drove down instead of catching the train."

"Well, it's their first grandchild. They're excited." Matt noticed Charlotte slipping off to sleep. "Do you want to sleep over, sis?" Charlotte jolted awake. "I can make up the spare room if you like?"

"No, I'll set off back in a few minutes. I'm exhausted, and the busy season of babies and weddings hasn't even started yet." Charlotte stretched her arms out as she yawned.

"How long is it until the wedding?" David asked.

"Nine weeks," she said. "And six weeks until little Ivy comes."

"If she comes on her due date," Matt said. "She could come any time now really, or be late. It's like a ticking time bomb. Whenever my phone pings I'm having a miniature heart attack."

"It's true," David said. "I set the smoke alarm off the other day and this one almost gave birth himself."

Matt playfully hit David on the arm.

"What's the plan for when she's born then?" Charlotte asked. "Do you wait here and they bring the baby to you? How does it all work?"

"Well, the mother is in Chester, so once we get the call we will go straight there and stay in a hotel near the hospital. Social Services have arranged for a room to be on stand-by for us. The mother will get some time with Ivy if she chooses and we just wait for the social worker to call us to say we can go to see her. Then, if all is well with the baby, she can come out with us straight away."

"Wow, you guys are having a baby." She beamed. "I still can't believe it. Even Hema and Mark have been inspired by your baby fever and have been discussing their future plans. Everyone is growing up."

They all sat in a joyful silence for a moment before David offered to make them all a coffee.

"Just a small one," Charlotte said. "I'll have to get home. I need to reply to Ross too, he sent me a message earlier." She pulled out her phone.

"Anything exciting? You should have invited him."

"Oh, I think he had book stuff to do today," she lied. "He just messaged to send his best wishes for the party."

"I'll go help with the drinks so you can reply to him." Matt collected a few more empty glasses and carried them into the kitchen.

Charlotte wondered what to reply to Ross, it had been a few hours since his message.

Today was perfect, she typed. *Everything went to plan. Are you free for a phone call one evening next week? X*

His reply came almost instantly.

> I'm so glad to hear it :) I can call you on Wednesday? I miss your voice. We can make plans for the weekend Xx

> Sounds like a plan, speak to you then X

She kept her phone in her hands thinking back to the news Mark had presented her with. Sam wanted to speak to her. Should she send him a message? Does he deserve to hear from Charlotte after all this time? What could he possibly have to talk to her about?

CHAPTER 25

By the middle of Charlotte's week, something didn't feel right. For a few nights, she had been woken up every hour, but she didn't know why. There was no noise, she wasn't having any bad dreams, but almost on the clock, something was waking her up.

At work, things still felt odd. She checked through the paperwork on her desk, all was fine. She reread her emails, wondering if she had forgotten to call any parents back, but there were not any scheduled calls or appointments. She looked at the wall calendar, but there was nothing she had missed, but something felt off. What was it?

She left her office and wandered down to Bananas, which was the baby room. Most of them were having their midday naps, with one unsettled and in the arms of Lilly who was softly singing to try to soothe her. Other than that, everything was fine there.

She then went into Apples to check with the staff that everything with the toddlers was okay.

"Yep," Humaira said. "We've got them all in their highchairs for their lunch which should be here any minute."

"Good stuff." Charlotte smiled at all the chubby little faces staring at her whilst kicking their chunky legs waiting eagerly for their lunches. They were babbling loudly to each other and hitting their hands on the empty trays in front of them.

She left and as she approached Strawberries, she realised what was wrong, what was missing. It was Wednesday and she'd not been called down to Strawberries to help out with Harrison. When Harrison was in Apples, Charlotte was usually called down there several times a day to help calm him, but ever since Emma started and he was moved up to Strawberries, there had been no problems. Rather than walk in, she glanced through the pane of glass in the door.

All the children were spread out around the room. Some were sitting on the carpet listening to a story, some were by the dressing-up box, and there were a few around the crafts table. This is where Harrison was, with Emma by his side. He was busy painting a picture and Charlotte was amazed to see that he was sharing the paints with the other children. He was calm, he was smiling, and all the children seemed relaxed around him.

Chloe saw her looking and opened the door to let her in. "Is everything okay?"

"Yeah, I won't come in, I don't want to disturb anything. I was just checking everything was okay."

Chloe glanced at Harrison. "Do you know what, everything's perfect. The change in him the last couple of weeks is unbelievable, don't you think?"

It was like music to Charlotte's ears. "Yes," she agreed. "It really is. I'll get back upstairs, I just felt like a little wander. I'll chat to you in a bit."

She walked back to her office and sat back down, tapping her fingers at her desk. There was still something missing, but she couldn't work out what it was. It felt as though there was an empty bubble of cloud in her mind.

And then it came to her. Sam. She still hadn't decided whether or not she wanted to speak to him. What would she say?

CHAPTER 26

*C*harlotte had some time to kill before her phone call with Ross. She had a quick shower after a jog with Matt and had a light tea before cleaning up and wondered what to do next. She had ordered a new book from Amazon which had arrived in the post that day and was sitting on her bedside table. It was the latest romance novel to hit the shelves. She was excited to start it but wanted to wait until after their call was finished so she could read until she fell asleep.

She had decided that she would take Hema's advice and invite Ross to her place for their next date. If she was going to imagine any kind of romantic future with him then she needed to see him in her normal, everyday life and not just in a romantic setting where everything was unrealistically perfect, because Charlotte was not perfect. She had faults and flaws just like everyone else and he needed to see that.

As she stood in her home office she stared at her desk where she had left her book plan. Ross had not made too many notes, but she still couldn't believe he'd given such positive feedback. Was he just being kind? Or did he genuinely enjoy it?

Without thinking about it, she switched on her new

Chromebook, opened a new Microsoft Word document and started tapping away. It hadn't taken long to download Microsoft the previous week, she was surprised at just how easy it was. The words flowed from her fingertips, like they had been waiting and waiting to come out and fill the white blank pages in front of her. Forty minutes after switching her computer on, she had the first three chapters of her book written. It wasn't much, but it was finally forming into something real that she could work on.

She sat back to read it, and read it again and again. Just as she was about to begin the fourth chapter, she heard her phone ringing from the living room so quickly sprinted across the hallway to answer it.

"Hello," she said, smiling at seeing Ross's name on the screen.

"Hello, Charlotte," he said.

"Hey." She smiled at hearing his voice. She loved hearing him say her name. "How are you? Have you had a good day?" She walked back into her home office and sat on the desk chair.

"A really good day, my publishers have sent back the manuscript today which is great, so I have a few edits to do, but I've told them I'm busy this weekend so they may need to wait until the new year. I was thinking about where we could go."

"Oh yes?" She wondered how to broach the subject of a night in at her place.

"I thought we could go to York for the day. We could walk along the city wall, find all the antique book shops hidden away in the old streets. There's a lovely Italian restaurant I want to take you to–"

"Actually…" It was now or never. "I had another idea. Why don't you come over to mine? I'd like to cook for you."

"A night in?"

"Yes, nothing rude, I promise." She laughed nervously. "But I just thought we could keep it low-key and I could treat you for a change."

"That sounds…" She was worried he wouldn't like it. That it

was not romantic enough for him. "Perfect. I would love to see your place. Shall I bring the wine? What's your preference?"

"Anything, I'm not fussy when it comes to wine." She felt very relieved that he had accepted her plan. A day out in York sounded wonderful, especially with antique book shops on offer, but something more intimate was needed to see where their relationship was going and how she really felt about him.

"I'm looking forward to it," he said. "We can go to York nearer Christmas for the markets if you like? What time would you like me to arrive on Saturday?"

They finalised their arrangements for the weekend and it was agreed Ross would also bring dessert.

"So how was your day?" he asked. "Anything exciting happen?"

"No, work's been very calm lately." She wondered if she should mention her sleepless nights, or Sam's request for her to reach out to him. "Oh, I did start writing just before you called. I've actually written the first three chapters of my book. The words just came from nowhere, but I'm staring at them now on the computer screen." She couldn't believe that her decade-old plan was finally taking shape. It was rough, of course, but finally springing into life.

"That's so exciting! I knew you could do it. Why don't you send them to me?"

"Oh, well, I've literally just written them," she said. "I doubt they're any good."

"Please, email them across to me. I'll text you my email address, I'm so excited to read your work. And I could give you some tips on direction."

She promised to send them across, scared at the thought of anyone reading them, never mind L. Rosebud himself!

They ended their call and Charlotte sent her chapters to him as promised, her finger quivered as she clicked the send button. No turning back now!

CHAPTER 27

"*A*re you going to sleep with him?" Hema loaded their plates into the dishwasher after joining Charlotte for a Friday night of food and wedding prep. It was time to put together the wedding favours which was soon becoming a tedious task. They had over a hundred miniature paper boxes to fold so they could be filled with sugar-coated almonds.

"No," she said instantly, losing a battle with one of the boxes she was trying to fold whilst Hema cleaned up. "That's not the plan. You were right, I need to see him on my territory. It might be the best way to figure out how I feel about him. I mean, he's absolutely perfect. He's the poster boy for dating and the kind of guy I should be with. I'm always excited for our phone calls and being with him feels so right. I just don't know where my head is at."

Hema popped a tablet in the compartment and closed the dishwasher.

"Have you shaved?"

"No, I told you, I won't be sleeping with him." It was weird to think about having sex with anyone in a bed she'd shared with

Sam for so long, although it had been a long time since they'd had sex or even hugged in that bed, or any bed for that matter.

"Still, just in case. What if you decide that you do really like him, and then the opportunity presents itself after a few glasses of wine and suddenly you're self-conscious because you can plait your foof?"

"It's not that bad!" She threw a badly folded box at Hema.

It couldn't hurt to be prepared, she thought, and decided that her Saturday morning would be a full on pamper session, consisting of body hair maintenance and exfoliation. She wouldn't tell Hema that though.

They spent the rest of the evening having a *Sex and the City* marathon while going over table plans and rearranging where guests were sitting away from Mrs Patel's controlling gaze.

"So, Mark said he saw Sam the other week, and that he's been wanting to talk to me."

"Yes." Hema looked up. "I'm sorry I didn't say anything. We weren't sure if it was too soon or what."

"Don't apologise, it's fine. It just surprised me, you know? I haven't heard from him at all since he moved out. Not even a text, but now he wants *me* to call him? Why can't he just man up and call me?"

"I said the same thing to Mark," Hema nodded. "Your entire relationship was based around you doing everything. If he wants to speak to you that much, why can't he bloody do something about it? It's not like he doesn't know where you live. Couldn't he send a letter? Why drag Mark into it? Does he even help out with payments for this place?"

"He puts money into my account every month towards half the rent, nothing for the bills, but we've never even discussed the tenancy. It's still got a few more months so I guess when it's renewed in just my name he can stop making payments."

"Would you move somewhere else?"

Charlotte had considered somewhere more affordable, but

she had made this place her home. She couldn't imagine living somewhere else now, although the memories of happier times still lingered in certain areas. In the bathroom where he would surprise her with candle-lit bubble baths after a stressful day. In the bedroom where his attempt at changing the bedding caused such a mess they always ended up in a fit of giggles. Not forgetting the lounge when they first moved in before they'd bought a couch and had to use their pillows to create a makeshift seating area, eating Chinese noodles from takeaway boxes and fiddling with the TV ariel to get a clear signal.

"One day, maybe," she said. "It might be nice to have a fresh start somewhere new, just mine."

"Somewhere new sounds like a good idea."

Hema left later that evening and told Charlotte to keep her updated on whether she decided to contact Sam or not, and to report back on her date with Ross, which is what she was most excited to hear about.

CHAPTER 28

*T*he countdown was on. Ross would be there any moment and Charlotte was nervous. She had pampered herself and put on a knee-length black dress with a mauve cardigan, not wanting to give the wrong impression by showing off too much flesh. To calm her nerves, she had allowed herself a small glass of wine as she tried to envision a relationship with Ross. What would it be like?

He was incredibly kind and generous, clearly wanting to spoil her. Who doesn't secretly want that? He had taken her to some amazing places for their dates, well and truly sweeping her off her feet. Chivalry was not something she was used to, but it came so naturally to Ross. Not forgetting that he lived a literary life and loved how much she adored reading and encouraged her passion for writing. A partner who loved books as much as she did was a good thing, wasn't it? From a physical point of view, he was very good looking. Exactly her type, and he was a very good kisser. There was potential for a very satisfactory physical relationship.

Her thoughts then went to Sam and how their relationship had turned out. They had very little in common in the end. No shared passions. He had changed so much, not just his attitude but his appearance too. And now he wanted to speak to her, to see her. What did he have to say? Was he sorry? Did he want to try and fix things? What did he want?

Knock-knock.

She checked herself in the mirror, flicking her hair behind her shoulders, and walked steadily to the door.

His smile almost knocked her back. In all her anticipation, she had forgotten just how attractive he was, and what his smile could do to her.

"Good evening. Wow, you look amazing." Ross stepped inside as she closed the door. He kissed her cheek and passed her a bag. "I wasn't sure what food you would be serving, so I brought three different wines to be sure. And I called at a patisserie earlier and picked up a selection of desserts so you can choose what you would like. They're in here." He held up a paper bag and she took them from him too.

He was incredibly thoughtful, she thought. Another positive trait for a potential boyfriend.

"This is great," she said. "Come through to the kitchen."

He followed her down the hall, looking around and taking in his surroundings.

"This place is great," he said. "Very homely, I love it. Is that your office?"

Charlotte cursed herself for not closing the door properly.

"Can I go in?" he asked.

"Sure," she said, apprehensively. She quickly put the wine on the kitchen counter and the desserts in the fridge then rushed back out to follow him.

He stepped inside and looked around. "So, when do you plan on opening up your own library?" He laughed. "This is *amazing*. I don't think I've ever seen such a collection in someone's home before. You'll need an extension soon if you buy any more. Let's see who you've got in here."

He trailed his fingers along the books, calling out authors names he approved of. Most of whom he had met personally over the years. He also pointed out which authors' names were made up for the purpose of publishing, referring back to their first conversation about authors using pen names.

"Honestly, I can't get over the amount of books you have. It's breathtaking."

"I can't help myself," she said, eyeing up her collection. "If I see a book I might enjoy then I *have* to buy it. Too many times I've put books back, telling myself to get it another time but by then I've forgotten what it was and instantly regretted not just buying it in the first place."

"Always let yourself buy the books. Never stop. Life's too short." Ross smiled at her. Charlotte remembered how Sam would tut every time she came home with a new book or had an Amazon delivery. And how the real reason she stopped herself buying more was to avoid his disapproval. "You've got some great books here, have you read them all?"

"I have." She stepped in the room to be near him. "Some I've read twice. And then these ones..." She pointed towards the L. Rosebud books which had their own section. "These have definitely been read more than once."

"They must be good then," he teased, raising an eyebrow.

"Meh, they're all right I suppose, if there's nothing decent to watch on television."

"Cheeky." He pulled her close and they kissed. Charlotte hadn't meant it to happen, but it happened so naturally.

Good kisser, definitely a pro to being boyfriend material. In fact, change that to amazing kisser.

As she pulled away, she could see he wanted more, but being the gentleman, he didn't push her.

"Shall we get a drink?" she suggested.

She led him into the kitchen where the dining table had been set for their dinner. Placemats which had been in long-term hibernation had been scrubbed and cleaned and placed on the table along with silver candle holders and polished cutlery.

"Your table setting's beautiful," he said. "I love the candle holders."

"Thanks, they belonged to my grandma. I'm not sure how old they are but I always admired them so she made sure they were given to me in her will."

"Well both you and your grandma had great taste."

Complimentary about her efforts, another pro.

"Thank you." She smiled as she looked over the bottles of wine. "I'm not sure which of these would be best," she confessed. "I'm not much of a connoisseur when it comes to wine."

He joined her at the counter. "What have you made for dinner?"

"I've made bruschetta to start, and we have carbonara for our main."

"This one then." He pulled out one of the white wines. "Definitely this one."

The food had been a huge success and Ross had been sure to compliment her culinary skills and insisted on clearing the plates away whilst she sat back and enjoyed a glass of wine. When he finished clearing away, he sat back down with her at the table and topped up their drinks. They had talked the whole evening, covering almost everything they could possibly talk about, more than they had in their previous dates, which proved to Charlotte that an intimate night in with just the two of them was the best way to properly relax in Ross's company. They'd discussed childhoods, families, favourite holidays, where they each wanted to travel to. Chat then turned to Charlotte's book collection and the ones they had both read so they could discuss them in detail, what they liked and disliked about a particular plot or character.

Charlotte could see they had a lot in common and felt a lot more confident moving forward in their potential relationship and was beginning to open up to him, although she left Sam out of the picture, not wanting to taint anything.

Charlotte asked what was planned for the launch of the next L. Rosebud book and was pleased to hear there were plans in place for him to go on a book tour of the Waterstones stores again.

"Another author event is great," Charlotte said. "Will there be another one around here?"

"There should be, I insisted. Seeing as though the last one led me to you." Ross placed his hand on Charlotte's. Their fingers intertwined, and she felt things she hadn't felt in a long time.

"Shall we go sit in the lounge?" she suggested.

"I'd love to." He picked up their glasses and followed Charlotte as she led the way into the lounge, taking a seat beside her on the sofa. There was music playing softly in the background. "So, I read your chapters." He put the drinks down on the coffee table and then put his arm around her.

"Oh, I'd forgotten all about that," she lied. Truthfully, she'd not stopped thinking about it, worried about what he would think about her attempt at writing. Would he humour her? Would he tell her gently that she didn't have what it takes?

"Charlotte," *Here it comes*, she thought. "You have such a gift. You need to write this book. There is so much passion in your words, when I finished the last page I just," he looked into her eyes. "I didn't want it to stop. I wanted to read more."

Charlotte blushed. "You don't need to be so nice, if there is anything to criticise, please tell me."

"I have no criticism. Only that I may now have competition."

They both laughed, and Charlotte noticed he was getting closer. His other hand edged towards her leg, his face just inches from hers. They were going to sleep together. She had created the perfect environment for them to spend the night together, and why not? They were both single, they both liked each other, he was absolutely perfect and definitely boyfriend material. Why shouldn't she take things to the next level? His hand reached up to her cheek, and he pulled her closer to him. What was stopping her?

"Stop." She almost startled herself at the sudden, unexpected outburst.

He jumped back. "Is everything okay?"

Something inside her was telling her this was a bad idea. As soon as she'd closed her eyes and leaned forward to kiss him, she saw Sam's face staring back at her.

"It's too soon," she said without thinking.

"We can take things slow, it's absolutely fine. I'm sorry if I was rushing you there..." he shuffled back to give her some space.

"You weren't." She wished he would stop saying all the right things. "I'm so sorry, I just can't do this, any of this, yet."

At their first date, she had been vague about her relationship with Sam, not wanting to be the girl that could only talk about her ex-boyfriend. He knew the basics, that their break-up was the push she needed to make some changes and become herself again, but that was all. He had mentioned his own previous relationships which had ended as he had been establishing his writing career but he was now ready to settle down with the right woman.

"It's too soon for you, I understand."

He was caring and considerate, another unfortunate pro.

"Come here." He held out his arms and she fell into them, allowing his kind hugs to comfort her. She was fighting back the tears she had been spending so many months holding back, not wanting to cry in front of this wonderfully caring man.

"I'm sorry." Her voice was muffled. "I really wanted to. I thought..."

"Don't apologise, please. You have nothing to be sorry about. I think it's just very bad timing."

He held her for a few more moments before allowing her to pull away. They both stood, not quite knowing what to say.

"I can stay if you want a friend with you this evening. If you need to talk about anything, it might help. I have a good shoulder, you know." He smiled.

"No, I'll be fine, thank you." She smiled back. It was all she could do at that moment.

She followed him to the door where, she suspected, it would be the last time she saw him.

"Please." He stepped back into the flat. "Please carry on writing. I mean it, your book has huge potential. You have a talent, don't let it go to waste."

He brushed a stray hair from her face and gently stroked her damp cheek. They said their goodbyes and he turned away from her, walking down the steps towards his car.

After she locked the door, she walked into her bedroom wanting nothing more than her big, comfy pyjamas and dressing gown. They were extra baggy as they were from her pre-diet days, but big pyjamas were the best for comfort. She reached for her red tartan pyjama bottoms which fell to the floor. She noticed something else had fallen out of the pocket.

Charlotte picked up the silver pendant necklace Sam had gifted her at their graduation, and the photo of them looking happy and in love, from the floor. She had shoved them both in there so they were out of sight. Before she knew it, she was curled up in her bed, clutching the photo and necklace and crying into her pillow.

She had no choice now. It was time to message Sam.

CHAPTER 29

*O*nce she composed herself and wiped away the last of her tears, Charlotte returned to the couch and sat by herself in a trance until the ping of the dishwasher finishing its load distracted her. Her mind had been going over everything that had happened that year. From starting out in an established relationship to then being single. To meeting an amazing man and then not being able to take it any further. She had been so close to something happening with Ross. So close, but something inside stopped her. Something deep down made her realise that it didn't matter how much she liked Ross, and how much she wanted to take things further with him. Charlotte knew that one thing was missing. Closure.

She had no doubt that ending things with Sam was the best thing she could have done. She was more confident in herself, she had lost weight, and she was taking steps to writing her first book like she had wanted to do all those years ago. All things she wouldn't have achieved if Sam was still in the picture. She looked to the armchair he always sat in that she could never bring herself to sit in or even throw out, but remembered the old shorts he would always wear whilst he sat there to either play on his games console or his phone, never taking an interest in her or what she was doing.

Charlotte then thought to all the places she had been out that year. Bolton Abbey, Ilkley, romantic restaurants and how there was no way Sam would ever want to go anywhere like that with her, let alone suggest it. So why was he still a barrier to her happiness? It was time.

She typed the message out in her phone.

> Hi, I hear you bumped into Mark and wanted to speak to me.

Charlotte kept it blunt, and his reply was almost instant.

> Hi! Thank you so much for texting me. Yes, please can we meet? I have so much to tell you.

Charlotte couldn't deny she was curious.

> Okay, I can do next Thursday after work.

> Shall we meet at Starbucks in town? I can't wait to see you.

> Starbucks is fine, I'll see you about 6.

His enthusiasm to meet her only added to the curiosity. Had he really missed her that much? They'd not seen each other for nearly eight months. Even texting him felt strange. Charlotte wondered if he'd been seeing anyone else in the time they'd been apart, like she had been seeing Ross. She tried to picture Sam kissing someone else. She couldn't.

Once that was arranged, she wondered if she should send a message to Ross to apologise again, but she figured enough had been said. She'd had her chance, but it was no good. She had no feelings for Sam, she was sure of that, but maybe meeting him was the best way to let go. She decided instead to send a message to Hema to fill her in on the evening's turn of events. Hema's reply was also instant.

> Aw Charlotte. Do you want me to come over? I've had a drink (don't tell Mrs P!!) but I can get a taxi? Xx

> No, I'm fine honestly. I just want to get into bed. Just wanted to update you xx

> Okay, call me anytime and I'll come over. I hope you're ok, sounds like there's a lot going on in your head Xx

> Nothing a good sleep shouldn't sort out. Not meeting Sam till Thurs, so I can update you then xx

> Okay, I'll speak to you before though to make sure you're okay. Do you think you'll speak to Ross again soon? Xx

> I doubt it... bad timing and think I've probably ruined it now. He was great about it, but it's not fair to mess him about xx

Charlotte went into the bathroom and saw the bags under her eyes. Tonight there would be no reading, no film, no phone. She knew that once she got into bed, the best thing for her would be a long, long sleep.

CHAPTER 30

*C*harlotte arrived at work unusually early on the Monday morning. Having not slept very well since her rendezvous with Ross and feeling incredibly guilty at the prospect of leading him on with the possibility of a relationship only to let him down as things began to turn physical. Her mind had also been spinning with thoughts of Sam and why he was so eager to see her. Where had he been for almost a year? What was he doing? Where was he living? Had he been missing her? Had he made any changes to his own life? Was he exactly the same?

All of her thoughts and questions were tearing through her mind, leading her to forget what she was doing. It was also the reason she accidentally drove through a red light on her way to work. Luckily, the roads were quiet at the time she had set off for work that morning, so no harm was done so long as she didn't get a ticket through the post.

"Why am I in the cellar?" she asked herself out loud, wondering why she was staring into a cold, dark room the nursery used to store old toys, props and… "Christmas." She finally remembered. The first Monday in December meant getting ready for the festive season. The children, especially the older ones, always got excited when they saw the first signs of Christmas and spent a lot of their craft time making ornaments to decorate the trees with.

Charlotte single-handedly pulled all of the artificial trees upstairs and into their allocated rooms. Each room was also given a box of tinsel and garlands that the nursery practitioners could use to decorate the walls and windows as they wished. Charlotte never dictated this, deciding it should be personal to each room, and the children were free to make their own festive decorations too, which they were allowed to take home on the last day before the nursery closed for Christmas.

By the time she was finished moving everything upstairs she felt like she had done a workout, and it wasn't even 8am yet. Her stomach growled angrily, as though scolding her for not giving it a proper meal since Saturday's carbonara. Once all the staff had arrived, Charlotte decided she would see how many of them fancied a breakfast sandwich from the café over the road. It would be her treat.

Chloe was the first to arrive.

"Woah." She looked at all the boxes clogging the corridor. "You've been busy. What time did you get here?"

"A little before seven." She pulled a tissue from her pocket to wipe the sweat from her forehead. She also needed to hoist her trousers up as they were far too loose on her. Charlotte knew this meant another scolding from Mrs Patel for losing yet more weight.

"Are you all right?" Chloe asked. "You don't look too well this morning."

"I'm fine," she lied. "Didn't get much sleep this weekend so decided to stop fighting it and got up extra early this morning."

"Not much sleep, ey?" Chloe smiled. "Must have been a good date with the author on Saturday. How did it go?"

Charlotte shook her head, trying to hold back tears. "I'd rather not talk about it."

"Ah, erm." Chloe got the message. "Look, why don't you go home today? There are plenty of us in."

"No, I have too many emails and telephone calls to potential new parents to make today."

"Take the laptop home and work from there, you can be undisturbed then."

"No, honestly it's fine." She picked up one of the boxes. "I could do with the distraction. And what better excuse is there than Christmas?" Charlotte managed a smile.

"Okay, but I'm helping you with these and then you're having a break with a brew for a while. No arguments."

"Actually, I'm going to treat everyone to a breakfast this morning from over the road so I'll hang on a little bit for a drink."

"You'll still have time to sit down with a brew, the kids aren't all usually in and settled until half nine. Come on, I'll help with these and then put your feet up before madness begins."

Over the years, the staff at the nursery had grown close. Most of the practitioners were in their early twenties so Charlotte had come to think of them as her little sisters, but right now she needed to talk to her big brother. She knew he'd want to know what was going on, and he would know what she needed to do, so once all the decorations were sorted and hot breakfast sandwiches had been distributed and consumed, she found her phone to give him a call. When she picked up her phone though, she saw she had three missed calls from him already.

"Charlotte!" Matt sounded out of breath as he answered on the first ring. "I was just about to try calling you again."

"Is everything all right?"

"Oh my God, you won't believe it, we're packing."

Packing? Charlotte wondered why. They wouldn't be going on holiday now, would they? Unless they had decided on a pre-baby getaway.

"Why, where are you off to?"

"Chester!" he almost cried. "The social worker just called us barely an hour ago. Ivy is on the way so we have to go now. David's getting some things ready for her and I'm about to phone my clients to let them know I won't be available for a few weeks. And I've already forgotten the name of the hotel the social worker told me so I need to call her back to check."

"Oh my God, Matt." Charlotte was almost crying herself. This was definitely a welcome distraction to her troubles. "Your baby is on the way!"

"I know, and early too. You know I like efficiency, but we feel so unprepared for this."

"You're more than prepared, I'm so excited for you both. Do you need me to do anything?"

"Yes, I do, if you don't mind?"

"Of course I don't, anything, you name it." Charlotte imagined he was going to ask her to make sure their fridge was stocked up in time for their return. Perhaps grab a few essentials, make some phone calls. Their parents would need to know for sure.

"Can you run the class for me tomorrow?"

"Can I… you want me to…" Charlotte was very good at rallying and organising toddlers when needed, she had even led the kids in a child-friendly workout a few times, but adults were a completely different audience. They would realise she was as coordinated as a Koala.

"Please, it's too late to cancel and I wouldn't want to let the ladies down anyway. We close for two weeks over Christmas and I don't want them waiting until January to meet up again. Can you do it? Please?"

"Of course I can," she decided. How could she not help him out? Matt had helped her so much this year so it was the least she could do. "I'm so excited to meet Ivy."

"And I can't wait to introduce her to Aunty Charlotte. Are you okay, anyway?" he asked. "How was your date?"

"Oh, I'll tell you about that when I see you. Your news is far more exciting than mine. Go on, go finish getting ready for your little bundle of joy. I'll speak to you later."

"All right, I'll call you when I have news. Love you, sis."

"Love you too."

Charlotte sat back in her chair. Her cup of tea from her earlier break had long since run out, but she didn't have the energy to get up and make another. Her brother was about to become a father, and in a matter of weeks, her best friend was getting married. So many big life changes happening around her and to the people she loved most in the world. When would it be her turn? She wondered what Ross was doing at that moment. Was he all right? Was he thinking about her?

Then, right on cue, her phone buzzed with a message. She hoped it was Ross, but it wasn't.

Are we still on for Thursday? Sam's message read.

He was certainly eager to see her.

Yes, I'll be there at 6

She wasn't sure how eager she was to see him.

CHAPTER 31

Start weight: 14st 7lbs
Current weight: 11st 3lbs

 rs Patel was going to go mad, Charlotte thought as she stepped off the scales. She suspected a few of those pounds would have dropped from three days of being too distracted to eat. She had arrived at the centre early so she could get herself weighed in first and then be free to meet and greet everyone else and explain why Matt was absent. There was not much that needing doing to prepare for the session, so she topped up her water bottle in the small kitchen and swiped open her phone to watch the video Matt had sent her in the early hours.

"Hello Aunty Charlotte," he said in the video. His eyes were bloodshot from a combination of emotions and exhaustion. "Let me introduce you to your niece."

The camera then panned across to a hospital crib, showing

Charlotte a tiny bundle all scrunched up in a floral baby grow with a matching hat. Ivy was asleep and totally unaware of how much joy she was bringing to her new parents.

The ladies began to arrive so Charlotte quickly put her phone away and went out to greet them. They were starting to form a queue at the weighing station.

"Hello, everyone," she said as she appeared.

"Oh, hello, love. Where's Matt?"

Matt had told Charlotte in their phone call the previous morning that she was allowed to share their exciting news with the group. He imagined they would be speculating about where he was, seeing as they had all been involved with his journey too.

"Well, once everyone is here, I'll explain, but he won't be here this week and possibly next week too."

"Is he ill?" one asked.

"Is he all right?"

"He's fine." Questions were being fired at her from the room, with only a handful of the ladies giving Charlotte a knowing smile. "Absolutely fine. I'll tell you all properly once we're weighed in and settled. Now, who's first today?"

🐌

"That's wonderful!"

"Congratulations to them!"

"We'll have to have a collection!"

"Congratulations to you too, Aunty Charlotte!"

"Thank you everyone," Charlotte smiled. "You all know, probably as much as I do, how much they've struggled to have a baby." There was a hum of agreement in the room. "They're still in Chester at the moment but once they're back I'm sure he'd love to hear from you all."

"What shall we do now then?"

"Shall we just go home?"

150

"Do we come next week?"

Charlotte jumped in. "Matt asked me to run the class for him but I'll be honest… I have no idea how to choreograph a dance. I wouldn't know where to start."

Charlotte felt like she was letting the group down. Like she was letting Matt down too in his hour of need. She didn't know what else to do.

"Can I help?" a woman in her mid-forties came forward. "I used to go to another Zumba class and they had a routine to 'Firework' by Katy Perry which they'd do at *every* session. I'll have it memorised for eternity. We could do that if you like? I have a workout playlist on my phone actually, I could try to put a few together?"

"Of course, that'd be so helpful!" Charlotte felt a surge of relief. "Is that all right with everyone?"

The group cheered and spread out to make room for a new Zumba dance. The woman, Claire, stepped forwards and connected her phone's Bluetooth to the speaker system and the music began to play. Charlotte took her place among the other women as Claire did an amazing job. She would be calling Matt that night to tell him the class was a success.

"Let us see the video again!" one of the older ladies called out before they all left.

Charlotte obliged so they could all see baby Ivy for themselves for a third time.

"Aw, adorable."

"Precious."

"Such a blessin'. You'll give him our love, won't ya?"

"I absolutely will," Charlotte promised. "Thanks so much for this evening everyone. Especially Claire, you're a lifesaver."

"Oh it's nothing," Claire smiled. "Glad I could help out. See you next week."

"See you next week," Charlotte said. "Bye, everyone."

All the ladies took their things and left, leaving Charlotte to lock up. She heard her phone buzz with a message.

Really looking forward to Thursday.

Sam was definitely eager to meet her, but why?

CHAPTER 32

Charlotte's new uniform in yet another small size was delivered to the office on Thursday afternoon. She'd had to pin her old trousers to hold them together and stop them falling down, so she was relieved to get the new pair which fit her perfectly. The T-shirt was a great fit too.

"You should have taken a photo of yourself back in March." Chloe commented. "Then you could've done a 'before and after' thing. Do we not have any photos of you from last year? Wasn't there some taken at Christmas?"

Before Charlotte could stop her, Chloe had sat down at the laptop looking through the media files where all the nursery's photos were kept from over the years.

"I don't think I want to see what I used to look like. I'll have been so–"

"Here! Oh wow, you need to see this."

Charlotte reluctantly walked round to where Chloe was sat and looked apprehensively at the screen.

Before her eyes was the staff photo from their Christmas party, when they'd gone to the local pub for a meal.

"My face..." Charlotte reached to her cheeks, letting her

fingers trail down her jaw line, which she noticed wasn't even visible in the photo. "I looked awful."

"No you didn't!" Chloe reassured Charlotte, seeing she was getting upset. "You never looked awful, but look at you now. Look at what you've achieved this year. This is huge. You've made a big, massive change. Several big life changes. You should be proud of yourself. This photo is a reminder of where you started."

"I am proud." Charlotte thought about it. "I can't remember the last time I felt this good." She looked down at her body.

"Good! Look to the future now. No going back to the old days."

Maybe not, Charlotte thought, but she was only a few hours from her reunion with Sam, and she had no idea what that would mean for her.

❦

Charlotte decided against getting changed into her normal clothes to go and meet Sam. It was only to Starbucks after all, and the winter chill meant it would be unlikely she'd be taking her coat off anyway. The drive-through windows were constantly open which meant it was usually cold inside. She already knew she'd be ordering a hot chocolate. It was dark by the time she set off from work into town. The sky was clear and the full moon was casting a white glow on all the trees.

This particular Starbucks had its own car park so she wouldn't have far to walk luckily. She couldn't see Sam's old Fiesta anywhere so assumed he was running a bit late, which suited her as she was feeling quite nervous. What would she feel when she saw him? Would she get upset? Would she be happy to see him? She had no idea, but her thoughts again went to Ross. Was he all right?

She swung open the door and was surprised to feel it was warm inside. The heaters were blowing from above.

There were quite a few people seated but still plenty of tables available. She decided to order her drink first. Service could be quite slow so if Sam turned up whilst she was waiting she could order his too to save time. She didn't plan on staying there too long. It was really warm inside though. Feeling flustered, she decided to take her coat off first.

"Oh, sorry," she said to the man behind her as she accidentally swung her arm back and knocked his chest.

"Ha-ha, probably the least I deserve. It's nice to see you."

Charlotte looked at the man she had hit with her arm. There was something familiar about him.

He was tall. A long, Parka coat stretched down to his knees but showed a very trim figure. Under it, Charlotte could see he was wearing a white shirt, unbuttoned at the top. Black suit trousers with black patent leather shoes. His dark hair was styled neatly, and his chiselled jawline was just visible under his black stubble. Then he smiled at her, and Charlotte knew that smile.

"Sam."

Sam insisted that Charlotte go and find a table and he would bring over their drinks. She did as she was told and chose one of the smaller tables in the far corner so they could sit opposite each other and she could get a good look at him. She watched him as he stood by the counter waiting for their drinks. Was it the same man? The last time she'd seen him, he wouldn't have fit into that coat, never mind the trousers. He had clearly been on his own weight-loss journey.

When the drinks were ready, he brought them to the table and sat opposite her.

"Can I just say," he began. "You look amazing. Seriously, amazing."

"Thanks," she blushed, wishing she'd have got changed into something a little smarter than a work uniform. "So do you. You went on that diet then."

"Yeah, I decided it was time."

"You look so different, I just can't believe it," Charlotte said again. "What happened? Where've you been?"

"Charlotte, I need to explain." He began fiddling with his own fingers, just as Charlotte would do when anxious. "When you ended things with me, it was the wake-up call I needed. I was in such a slump and couldn't see a way out. I was being awful to you but I didn't have the willpower to stop. You tried to get me to change, I can see it now," his voice began to break as he stirred his drink to distract himself and clear his throat. "I promised you the world and I didn't deliver. I let you down."

"Sam–"

"No, please, let me talk. The day I moved my things out, I quit my job."

"You quit?"

"Yes, as long as I stayed there I was never going to amount to anything, I hated it. Then I looked in the mirror and I hated what I could see. And when I first slept alone without you by my side, I hated that too. I decided there and then that I could let myself fall into a bad place or I could make some changes." He took a sip of his drink. "I decided to find a new career that I was passionate about. I was going to lose weight and be happy and confident again. And I would do whatever it took to get you back."

It was a lot to take in. Charlotte picked up her own drink and sipped it, not wanting to burn her lips. She took a deep breath to calm herself, but her heart was pounding hard in her chest.

"So, what did you do to make these changes?"

"Well, I couldn't do it alone. Being back at my parents' house meant I could talk to my dad about things. He asked me what I'm good at, and that was easy. Computers. More specifically, web design. I created a brand-new website for his company and then his friend wanted one doing too. Word was spreading and suddenly I'm the director of *Wallace's Web Designs*. I've made my own empire and I love my job." His smile was infectious. "I even have my own assistant."

"That's amazing!" She smiled. "I'm so happy for you."

"It's great," he was smiling too, clearly proud of his growing empire. "She's just in the middle of rebranding all my social media accounts. I'm off the radar at the moment but I'll be back on there soon. Next on the list was my size. Since I had decent money coming in, I was able to join a gym and work with a dietician. The weight was dropping off. I had to throw all my clothes out and buy new ones. I had a meeting with a client this morning, hence the fancy white shirt and shiny shoes."

"You look fantastic, really different but so good."

"I haven't had a takeaway in months, I was sure Just Eat were going to send out a search party for me."

Charlotte could not remember the last time she had a takeaway either. Even when Hema would pop around for a night in, she always cooked something fresh.

"The last thing on the list was you."

Charlotte's hands were on the table. Sam reached out and held on to them, grasping them tightly like he never wanted to let go of them ever again.

"Charlotte, I messed up big time."

"It wasn't just you," she said. "It takes two to tango. We both fell into a slump…"

"No, you tried so much. You would always try to put a positive spin on things. Dumping me when you did was the best thing you could have done. It was the kick up the backside I needed. I didn't deserve you, but I want to know, is there any way, any way at all you would let us try again?"

Charlotte thought hard about his question. He had laid out all his flaws on the table. Not only that, he acknowledged them and did something to improve his life. A life they could have together. The life they were supposed to have nine years ago when they graduated.

And then she remembered their graduation day and the promises he had made to her of marriage, a home and her own career. Could they go back to how they used to be, or was it too late?

CHAPTER 33

The end of the week could not come quickly enough for Charlotte. She made sure all the jobs at the nursery were done. All emails had been followed up, all meetings finished and she would be ready to leave as soon as the last child was collected.

"Go home now," the girls had insisted. "We can close up."

Charlotte knew that if she were to leave early, something would go wrong, so she stayed until the end to be safe, but luckily there were no problems which required her to stay after hours. So, just before five o'clock, she allowed the girls to go home and she locked up, practically dancing to her car so she could head to her brother's house to meet the latest addition to the Hicks clan.

She pulled up on the drive. The house was surrounded in darkness as winter had officially rolled in, with just a glow coming from the living room window where Charlotte could see the windowsill filled with cards and flowers from friends and family offering their congratulations. Grabbing her bag and the gift bag from the boot, she ran to the door letting herself in with her key. Matt was in the living room cuddling a sleeping Ivy who was tucked up to him, like she was always meant to be there.

"Hey," Charlotte whispered, looking in awe at Ivy. "Oh my God, she's so tiny!"

Matt carefully stood up, clutching Ivy to him and making sure he would not lose his grip on her, before releasing one arm to hug his sister.

"Here, take her if you want."

"Are you sure? I don't want to wake her."

"It's fine, she won't wake up," he insisted as Charlotte removed her coat. Matt gently placed the baby in her arms, and then stretched out his own arms for some relief from sitting in the same position for hours.

"She's so teeny." Charlotte held her close, smelling Ivy's head which smelled of baby powder. "She's absolutely perfect, I'm in love already. Where's David?"

"He's in bed," Matt yawned. "We're taking it in turns to do night feeds at the moment, until we get into a routine. He wanted to see you but I told him to get his sleep as it's his turn tonight."

"And how's it going? I know it's early days, but is it all right?"

"It's amazing, do you want a drink? I'll tell you all about it."

They walked into the kitchen together. Charlotte could not take her eyes away from Ivy, but when she looked up she wasn't sure how she could have missed the mess when she had run through the kitchen and into the living room.

Covering the usually pristine kitchen counter was a bottle prep machine, steriliser and tubs of formula, with a bit of powder splattered around. The draining board was full of washed bottles and by the sink were more waiting to be washed. In front of the washing machine was a small basket filled with muslin cloths and the odd baby vest.

"Wow, what a transformation," she observed.

"Oh, I know, and can you believe David hasn't complained

once." David had very high standards when it came to cleanliness and organisation. Clearly a new baby meant all that went out the window. "In fact, now you're here I can pop these in the steriliser, would you mind?"

"Of course not, do what you need to. I'm happy to do baby cuddles for as long as necessary. That's what aunties are for." she said as she gently cradled Ivy.

"Thanks," he began popping them in the machine. "She doesn't like being put down at the moment, she prefers to sleep on someone. The midwife who visited us said that was fine and expected. Something about the warmth from our bodies."

"Oh, so a midwife has been to see you here?"

"Yes, she came this morning with the social worker. Routine stuff."

Matt explained they had visited together that morning and were more than happy with how the new family had settled in together since arriving home the previous day. The midwife did her routine checks so Ivy could be on the system properly and explained that a health visitor would be in touch the following weeks to arrange their routine visits as well.

Once Matt had cleaned the kitchen and made their drinks, they settled back into the living room to relax, just as Ivy started to squirm.

"She'll want a bottle," he jumped up after checking his watch. "I'll go make it. Would you like to feed her?"

"I'd love to," Charlotte had helped to feed the babies in nursery for years, but they were usually six months old and more and always wanted to grab the bottle from her. She had never fed a newborn baby before. This was a truly precious moment.

As Matt prepared the bottle in the next room, she cradled Ivy, tapping her bottom with one hand as she had heard of mothers doing before to help settle babies to sleep. It seemed to be working as Ivy stopped fussing, but once Charlotte stopped for a moment to scratch her nose, Ivy began to cry. It was the sweetest sound which did not bother her at all.

"I'm coming," Matt called from the kitchen, flustered. "One moment."

He ran in frantically, not wanting his baby to be upset for any longer than she needed to be. Charlotte took the bottle from Matt and gave it to Ivy. She took it easily, sucking on the bottle like it was her first ever feed.

"Just sit her up a bit," Matt instructed. "The midwife said to try to sit her up as much as we can when we feed her. It's supposed to limit trapped wind, or something." He rubbed his eyes, clearly exhausted from the last few days.

Charlotte carefully shifted Ivy in her arms to a comfortable position, but she never stopped drinking for a moment.

"She was hungry, wasn't she?" she laughed, amazed at how such a tiny being could drink so much.

"Wasn't she just. We're supposed to wake her every three hours to feed her but she never gives us chance," he laughed which forced him to yawn. "She is absolutely ready for her bottle and makes sure we know about it. If I didn't know any better, I would say she gets it from David."

Charlotte laughed as Matt sat down next to her and she pulled an empty bottle away.

"I'm scared to burp her," she admitted. "She seems so delicate, I don't want to hurt her."

"You won't, here," he passed her a clean muslin cloth. "She's good at passing wind, from both ends if you must know."

After just ten gentle taps on her back, Ivy let out a monstrous burp loud enough to impress a pub full of drunken, rowdy rugby players. Once settled, she fell back into a deep, carefree milk coma. Matt took out his phone and began writing notes of what time she'd fed and how much she'd had.

"Well, I can safely say that things are *very* different now," he said, slipping his phone back in his pocket and taking a sip of his coffee. "Last Friday, we were sipping cocktails in Leeds until three in the morning. Now I'm onto the hardcore, full-strength coffee, getting as much caffeine as I possibly can to get me past nine o'clock. Although I'm still seeing three in the morning."

"Ha-ha, I guess things do change as we get older, but for the better."

"Definitely for the better."

They sat in silence for a few minutes, listening to Ivy's long, deep breaths as her full, round tummy moved up and down.

"So, what's going on with you? How was it on Tuesday?"

"Really good," Charlotte recalled the weight loss session she was in charge of. "I've lost another three pounds."

"Fantastic! Well done. And how was the class?"

"Great," she said. "They're all so excited for you. Another woman led the Zumba because I just didn't have a clue. I think her name was Claire."

"Oh yes, she knows her stuff. I am glad it all worked out. So, what else is going on? How's the author?"

Charlotte had been dreading this question.

"The author is... no more. I had to end it on Saturday. It just wasn't... it just..."

"What's been happening?" Matt moved up closer to Charlotte on the couch and put his arm around her as she told him all about her date with Ross, followed by her meeting with Sam. "Wow, and here's me thinking I'd been on an emotional rollercoaster the last few days. Is that why you sounded a bit down on Monday? It felt like something was wrong but I was too distracted. Shall I dig out the Quality Street? I've got a tub I've been hiding from David for Christmas."

"No, no I'm fine," she kept her eyes on Ivy. "I just don't know where my head's at. Sam has made all these changes, changes I needed him to make nine months ago. He's turned into the guy I wanted him to be, and seems determined for us to get back together. I mean, I look at you guys having a baby. Hema is getting married. Would it be easier to go back to him seeing as though he's made the effort?"

"Is it enough, though?"

"What do you mean? Shouldn't it be? It's what I wanted out of him after all."

"Charlotte, yes he's made the changes. I'm sure he looks amazing, and with a decent career he'll have a decent income too. But when you saw him, did you want to get back with him? What did you feel for him? What was your first thought?"

"That he looked really good, like the version of himself he was *meant* to be."

"But…" Matt hesitated. "Is that enough for what you want and need now? When are you seeing him again?"

"I don't know." With her free hand, she wiped away the tear which had slipped down her cheek. "I told him I needed some time, but I can't keep him waiting."

"You absolutely can! Oops." Ivy squirmed in her sleep at the noise, so Matt lowered his voice. "How long has it taken for him to reach out to you? Trust me, you can keep him waiting."

And she did.

CHAPTER 34

Charlotte's mind was full of a mixture of emotions by the weekend. She was overjoyed at the long-awaited arrival of her beautiful, precious niece. Such a tiny bundle that had already brought so much happiness. Matt's daily WhatsApp photos of Ivy always made Charlotte smile. Charlotte was still overcome after her meeting with Sam just days before, not able to process her feelings or differentiate between what she wanted and what she needed. It was early December, and even though her best friend's wedding was just weeks away, she was also aware she would be facing spending the Christmas period alone for the first time ever.

It was Saturday and she had resisted the urge to visit her brother, deciding instead to allow the new family some precious time alone in their own bubble. Hema was also busy as her parents had whisked her and Mark away to visit some relatives in Leicester for some pre-wedding festivities.

To distract herself, Charlotte turned on the television, and the previous night's episode of *I'm A Celebrity, Get Me Out Of Here* was playing on ITV2. She had missed the first episode so decided to start them from the beginning on ITVX. Charlotte used to watch this every year. It was the highlight of her winter, but she had missed the last few series. As the opening titles began, she remembered why.

4 years earlier

"Ten famous faces are about to walk across this very bridge..."

"And ten famous faces have no idea what might be joining them in the jungle..."

"There will be trials and tests..."

"Possibly tears and tantrums..."

"And that's just us and the crew..."

"It's time to introduce them to you..."

"Here on I'm a Celebrity... GET ME OUT OF HEEEEEERE!"

The famous jungle drums began and Charlotte was ready. Late November meant she had the next few weeks of evening television to enjoy. She and Sam used to love watching this every year. It started as a tradition back in their final year of university together. Sam would buy the Chinese takeaway and Charlotte would supply a bottle of Malibu and Coke for the first episode and they would snuggle together under the duvet, but not anymore.

"Not this crap again." Sam entered the room and sat on his armchair.

"I've been waiting for it for weeks," the teaser trailers had got Charlotte giddy. And the rumours of which celebrities would be entering had been released the week before. "I can't believe the guy from *Hollyoaks* is going in, I love him!"

"There's always someone from bloody *Hollyoaks*, and Corrie, or someone from an old pop group needing money, and a sporting person no one's *ever* heard of who's always the first one voted out. Same shit every year. I don't know how you can stand it."

"I love it, you know I love it." It was rare Charlotte watched anything on television anymore thanks to work keeping her busy.

"It's always the same. Same kind of people, same bloody trials. It's boring. It's like *Love Island*. Just drains away brain cells. I could feel myself losing intelligence every time I heard the theme tune."

Charlotte used to love watching *Love Island* too. And *Married at First Sight*, *First Dates*. She would record all of those shows on their Sky Box to watch in the evening after work, but Sam's constant derogatory remarks, not letting her watch an episode in peace without making her feel bad, meant it was easier to just stop watching them at all. *I'm A Celebrity* was the last one she could get through without any comments. Or so it seemed.

"I'll bet you that guy's going to be this year's idiot," Sam said about the pop star as the screen showed the Australian villa where the first celebrities would meet each other. "Oh and she won't last long on rice and beans, look at the size of her! What about him? How's he going to get through sleeping on a hammock, he's about seventy."

Charlotte could barely hear the celebrities talking as they all met for the first time. Each being handed a colourful cocktail as they stood beside a shimmering blue swimming pool with Australia's stunning blue sky as a backdrop.

"Oh and here *they* come," he continued. "These two idiots. They could at least have new presenters every year to spice it up a bit."

"I like them," she missed their introduction over Sam's talking.

"You would." At that, Sam pulled out his phone and started

playing on a game. He had recently been able to connect it to his Xbox so was playing the new *Call of Duty*.

"Can you turn the volume down please?" she asked.

"Oh is it disturbing your precious Geordie duo? Turn that down, thought you wanted us to spend more time together, I can't... oh come on!" he shouted at his game, making Charlotte jump. "Got killed, stop distracting me," he aimed at Charlotte.

Sam's shouting at his game continued. As did the loud bangs and voices of his teammates booming through the tiny speaker of his phone. Charlotte couldn't hear a thing.

It was the same the following night, and the next, and the next.

In the end, it was easier to stop watching altogether for some peace.

CHAPTER 35

The twelfth of December meant Charlotte's final dress fitting for the wedding. She had lost over three stone since her measurements were taken for the first time earlier that year and it was safe to say she was a lot happier with her size now. She often glanced through her photo gallery on her phone to compare "then and now" photos, amazed at the difference. Even her wardrobe had been completely transformed. She was no longer covering up with baggy jumpers and dark clothes and even Mrs Patel complimented her polka dot peplum top when she arrived.

"Okay, two weeks until the wedding," Mrs Patel began. "Try this on now. If it does not fit, you will be cursed for all eternity."

Charlotte emerged from the downstairs bathroom and walked into the lounge, standing on the little podium in front of the tall mirror which Mrs Patel had bought for Hema to use on the wedding day. Hema stood in the doorway, unable to take her eyes off her friend.

"Why are you staring at me like that?" Charlotte asked.

"You just look so... so great. Like when we were back at uni." Hema's eyes glistened. "I'm so proud of you."

As Charlotte smiled at the unexpected compliment, her eye shed a tear which she was unable to wipe away as an oblivious Mrs Patel lifted her hands above her head at that exact moment to make sure there wasn't a stitch out of place, but it did not go unnoticed by everyone.

"Mama," Hema stepped into the room. "Why don't you go and make us a drink?"

"She can't have a drink in this," she gestured at the dress. "No spills. This will be packed away until the wedding now. It is *finally* ready."

"She'll take it off whilst you pop the kettle on, go on. I'll help her out of it and make sure it's hung up. Go on, go."

It took some convincing but Mrs Patel finally left the room which was all Charlotte needed to finally let her emotions go.

"Hey, come here," Hema pulled Charlotte's hand to get her off the podium and close to comfort her. "What's the matter? Don't you like the dress? Is everything okay?"

"The dress is perfect, it's beautiful. I just..." tears were running down her cheeks.

"Come on," Hema pulled her to the downstairs bathroom. "Take the dress off before it gets damp. Mrs Patel is in a good mood at the moment, we don't want to ruin it."

Charlotte carefully took the dress off and passed it to Hema who gently folded it over her arm.

"Come on, what's the matter?" Hema asked as Charlotte started to get dressed.

"I don't know," she said as she pulled her top over her head. "Things have been weird lately."

"Is it Sam? Have you arranged to see him again? What's been happening?"

"No, I haven't seen him. But he sent me a message this morning asking me to meet him again. He wants to take me out."

"What have you said?" Hema got some tissue and passed to Charlotte who was now fully dressed.

"Nothing. I haven't even spoken to him since I saw him."

"And what are you thinking?"

"I don't know." They walked out of the bathroom together and back into the lounge, sitting beside each other on the sofa after Hema placed the dress back on the hanger. "I don't know what I'm feeling. Seeing him was just so... it felt like going back in time."

"He looked good, then?"

"He looked amazing. No sign of those grotty, horrible shorts. He was proper suited up. Whole new wardrobe, new business, entirely new attitude." Charlotte smiled.

"Would you want to get back with him?"

Charlotte didn't know what to say.

At that moment, Mrs Patel re-entered the living room with a tray of tea and assorted biscuits. She saw the dress hanging neatly on the door.

"I'll take this upstairs now, so it is safe. Don't you be losing any more weight, okay?"

"I won't, I promise," Charlotte forced a smile.

Mrs Patel left the room.

"What do you think I should do? Do you think I should give him a chance?" Charlotte asked.

"Honestly? No," Hema said bluntly. "I don't think anyone can change that much. He can dress himself up as much as he wants, and put on a smile as much as he can and tell you all the things he knows you will want to hear. But I wouldn't trust him."

"No?"

"No. I think seeing him should have been the closure that you need. That you've *needed*. Now you can move on."

"I tried to date someone else," Charlotte's mind went to Ross. She often had his face in her mind, wondering what he was doing, what he was thinking. "It just didn't work though, I couldn't make it work." Charlotte picked up a rich tea biscuit and dunked it in her cup of tea, pulling it out before it could break and sink to the bottom of the cup.

"You don't even need a new relationship if you're not ready, just something new in your life to be your focus. What about this book you're writing?"

"What about it?"

"Why don't you carry on with writing your book? You said you'd made a start already. Why stop? Take time away from men and focus on what you want to do. I know you want to be a writer more than anything. Just do that for a while, you never know where it could lead."

Charlotte pondered over this idea. She had not written any more since those first three chapters, but the ideas were floating in and out of her head all the time. Maybe Hema was right, she thought. It was time to focus on herself.

CHAPTER 36

Charlotte returned home from a very hectic day at work. Father Christmas had paid the nursery a visit and it was her job to escort him from room to room and then assist the staff in calming the children and babies who cried, as most of them usually did at the sight of Santa. It always fascinated her that the children loved to sing songs about Santa, read stories about him and paint pictures of him, but once faced with the real deal, they were petrified. It didn't matter that he was handing them each a present, they just ended up in tears. She secretly found it hilarious.

By the time they had reached Strawberries, even Santa himself needed a break, but Charlotte was very surprised, and even a little bit emotional, when Harrison stood up in front of everyone to say, "Thank you for my present, Santa." His progress over the last few months was tremendous. He was in his final year at nursery before moving on to Primary School and Charlotte was sad that this would be his final Christmas with them. She wondered if he would remember them in years to come. If at any point during his adult life he would have flashbacks to being in their nursery, playing with toys, running outside in the playground or even in the soft playroom upstairs. She doubted many of them would remember much about their time there, but she hoped one day to see them all in their adult lives and how they turned out.

Once Charlotte had finished her evening meal and cleared everything away, she went into her office to choose a new book to begin that night, when she glanced at her new laptop. Since speaking with Hema she had not had chance to sit down and write, but how could she try to finish her book if she did not *make* the time? It was time to stop thinking about Sam, Ross, about everything. Before she had chance to consider what she was doing, she switched on the laptop and took a seat, pulling her notes out of one of the drawers and laying them out in front of her.

The machine came to life immediately, as though eager for her to begin. She was amazed at the speed of the device compared to her old PC which usually needed a few minutes to consider whether it wanted to turn on or not. She opened the Microsoft Word document saved to her drive and quickly read through what she had written so far. She gently tapped at the keyboard, not even needing to glance at her notes again, and the words just poured out of her, as if magically appearing on the screen. Tap tap tap tap tap. Without even looking at the keys, her fingers typed and typed as though they had been waiting for this moment. Waiting for the opportunity to get out the words which had been burning inside them.

Four chapters, then five. She relocated to the comfort of her couch, loving that she was not restricted to a desk and now had the freedom to move around. Chapters six and seven were then complete. She leaned back to massage her knuckles which were now feeling tender after reaching chapter eight, she realised it was almost midnight.

"How did that happen?" she wondered.

She made sure to save what she had written so far, promising herself she would be back on it the next night, and the next one after that too. The only noise around her was the bleep from her phone notifying her of a message.

Can we meet again? X

It was Sam.

CHAPTER 37

Start Weight: 14st 7lbs
Current Weight: 11st 0lbs

"I don't think Mrs Patel will mind that," Matt said as Charlotte stepped off the scales.

"I think I'll be safe from her wrath for now," she smiled. Charlotte slipped her shoes back on and rushed back over to David who was holding on to Ivy and chatting with the other women at the Keep Fit class.

"… and she will absolutely learn ballet and tap," David said to his congregation. "She's going to be a dancer just like her daddy, aren't you?" he kissed her gently on the head.

"How are we doing?" Charlotte asked, taking hold of Ivy as David gently passed her over.

"All good, she's just nodded back off." David gently stroked her head.

"Looks good on you, Char," one of the ladies said.

"Suits you, that does," said another. "When are you going to have one?"

Charlotte tried to ignore the remarks.

"I might just check her nappy," David said quickly. "Do you want to bring her over here and we can look?"

"Yes, of course, excuse us, everyone." They walked to one of the tables in the corner of the room and away from the cooing older women. "Here." She motioned for him to take Ivy to do his fatherly nappy duties, but he didn't take her.

"Oh, she doesn't need checking, I was just wanting to get you away from those old bats pestering you about having a baby. You've just got that gorgeous figure back, no need to fill it up again."

Charlotte laughed and thanked him for rescuing her.

"I know things have been tough," he said. "Sorry I haven't been around much. Matt's been filling me in but I've not been doing well in the friend department lately."

"Don't be daft, you've got a new baby to think about. You don't need my troubles on top."

"If you ever have any troubles, call us. Honestly, it doesn't matter what time of day. Now little Ivy is here at least one of us is awake throughout the night. Promise you'll call us if you need us."

"I promise," she gently rocked Ivy. "Are you going to make it to the wedding this weekend?"

"We'll make the ceremony for sure. We'll bring enough baby supplies to see us for the whole day, but we might just leave if we feel we have to. I think she'll probably sleep through it all anyway, she's been really good for us through the day. It's just at night where she's wired enough to pull an all-nighter."

"I remember the days when you and Matt were wired enough to pull an all-nighter. Like the time you didn't get home until 11am the next day."

"Oh God, yeah... and we had your cousin's Christening to go to. I was sick as a dog."

Matt joined them, putting his arm around David. "What are you laughing at?"

"The old days." David smiled at his husband.

Charlotte noticed how tired they both looked, but how it was overshadowed by their undoubtful joy at what they now had together as a family of three.

"Are you doing a Zumba sesh?" David asked.

"Nah, not tonight. I know it's the last meet up before the Christmas break but I've told them all it's just a weigh-in tonight. Look, they gave me these."

He showed them a large, pink gift bag which was filled with soft toys, clothes, board books and cards which they had all bought with money collected from everyone in the class. They were both touched by the generosity of everyone, not just from this class but their friends, colleagues, neighbours, everyone who had been so kind to send gifts.

"Okay well, as much as I want to cuddle and snuggle this beautiful creature all night, I'll let you have her back and I'll head off."

She passed Ivy back to David, careful not to disturb her.

"What are you plans tonight?"

"I'm going to carry on writing," she said. She had been busy writing every day after work from the moment she walked through the door until she took herself to bed late at night. "I've almost got a first draft written of my book and I want to carry on working on it, try to get it done before the weekend if I can."

They walked back to the chairs in the middle of the room and Charlotte put her coat on and threw her bag over her shoulder.

"Well, we should see you on Saturday," Matt gave her a hug. "But in case we don't get chance to chat much, what time are you coming over Christmas morning?"

"Christmas morning?" Charlotte asked. "What do you mean"?

"You're coming to us, aren't you?"

"No, don't be daft. You guys need to enjoy your first Christmas as a family."

"And we will, as soon as you get there. We're not letting you spend it alone," Matt demanded.

"Absolutely not," David agreed. "I've got it all planned out anyway. All three of us can take it in turns to see to Ivy but I'm doing a massive brekky, then we can open presents. Matt's sorting lunch but he has promised none of this diet stuff. We're enjoying the calories."

"Definitely," Matt laughed. "Besides, the wedding will be over by then so we won't need to worry about our waistlines. So, what time are you coming Christmas morning?" He repeated.

"I'll be there first thing," Charlotte smiled. "As soon as I wake up, I'll be over."

"Come Christmas Eve if you want? You can sleep over. I don't want you waking up alone."

Charlotte considered their invitation, wondering if she really did not mind waking up alone on Christmas morning for the first time in her life. It would be strange, maybe even a little bit sad, but the process of moving on meant making big changes like this and she felt it was something she had to do to seal shut, once and for all, her relationship with Sam.

"I'm sure, you guys enjoy your first Christmas morning together. I'll be over before all the good films start."

They all kissed goodbye and Charlotte headed for the door, to her car, and back to her home all alone, anticipating her looming next meeting with Sam.

CHAPTER 38

The final day of nursery before closing for Christmas was always fun for the children. Charlotte was grateful that they were closing that Wednesday lunchtime so she could have an afternoon of writing before spending all of Thursday pampering and making sure there were no last-minute emergencies before a full weekend of wedding ceremonies and parties.

The English ceremony on the Friday was all arranged. It was to be a simple service at the local Town Hall followed by food and celebrations at a country pub for the sake of Mark's elderly relatives. Charlotte was not attending that, and neither were any other friends. It would just be parents, grandparents and siblings. The main event was Saturday. Charlotte was glad that Mrs Patel had finally caved to allow Hema and Mark to do things their own way and not to overdo it with the guest list. It was going to be a perfect weekend. Charlotte still wished she had Sam to go with her as originally planned, but she was not going to let anything bring her down at her best friend's wedding. It would be a perfectly happy day, full of distractions.

She did wonder though, if Sam had taken her up on her offer

of going on a diet together, would she be alone right now? If they had both joined Matt's fitness class and had a laugh together doing Zumba. If they would have celebrated their weekly weight loss achievements, and then allowed themselves the odd cheat day each month. If they would have gone out on the weekends for long walks during the summer once the weather was better, or if they'd have taken up running together. Would his attitude have changed that much, or would he have eventually slipped back into old, negative habits.

Charlotte made sure every piece of Christmas themed artwork had been pulled down so they could return in January and not have to worry about taking down decorations. She made sure every piece was given to every grateful parent who would now have to display them on their own trees and fridges for the foreseeable future and she gave each member of staff a Body Shop goody bag before they left and they each piled Christmas presents onto her too. Even Mrs White had been thoughtful and brought her a gift as a thank you for all her help with Harrison. There were so many presents that Chloe had to help her to her car.

"Have a good one," they each said as they departed.

Charlotte was excited to be spending Christmas day with her brother, David and baby Ivy, with a promised visit from their parents too who were travelling down from their home in the north east. It was going to be a magical day, especially just a few days after the wedding. Charlotte was secretly relieved that she wouldn't be spending the day alone after all.

On her way home, she called into Marks and Spencer to buy herself some supplies to see her through the next few days, which she regretted instantly as she saw the queues building at the tills. Luckily, she only had a few items so was able to rush through the self-serve checkout and back to the safety of her car away from people arguing over who got the last bags of sprouts and carrots.

She only just switched on the ignition when her phone began to ring.

"Hello?" she said to her dashboard as the Bluetooth connection kicked in.

"Charlotte?"

"Sam, hi." She turned off the car and put her phone to her ear.

"Are you still meeting me in town tomorrow?"

Charlotte allowed a few seconds of silence. She needed to speak to him, but it would need to be in person. "Yes, of course. I'll be there."

"Two o'clock? We can meet in the Waterstones café."

"I'll be there." Of all the places to have a serious conversation with him, he had to pick her favourite spot, and the place she remembers fondly from meeting Ross.

"Great, I can't wait, I'll see you tomorrow."

Sam clicked off the line before Charlotte could say any more.

CHAPTER 39

"*To record your voicemail, please speak after the beep.*"

"Hi, Hema," Charlotte began. "I've made it into Waterstones and it is crazy busy. There are psycho Christmas shoppers everywhere, I can barely move. I'm early so I'm going to have a wander first, there's a new Sophie Kinsella book I'm after which should be here somewhere. I'll call you again after I've spoken to him. You were right, and Matt was. I needed closure and I think I've had it. I'm going to tell him today. We *are* over, and he needs to move on too. Chat later."

Hema was clearly too busy to answer the phone, which was forgivable the day before her weekend of wedding shenanigans. She was probably being held up by Mrs Patel pestering her over something. Luckily, Charlotte was in her favourite place so didn't mind not having her friend on the phone to keep her distracted. She was in book heaven. Although it was not usually this busy, even at Christmas. Charlotte fought through the sea of bodies blocking her way around every turn making it difficult to get to the Romance section where she usually spent most of her time. The Christmas songs were barely audible over the sound of chatter and laughter.

"Oh, sorry," Charlotte said as she knocked into someone, forcing her to go the wrong way into Crime and Horror. She knew there was another way around to her destination via Travel but suddenly a large group of festively attired people appeared and were blocking her way, so she had to go back on herself. "What the..." she said out loud as the saw another group of tinselled up shoppers blocking the other way out.

As she looked around for another way out, she realised that every person around her was wearing something Christmassy. Some had elf hats, Santa hats or reindeer antlers. They all had tinsel around their necks and some with flashing lights, but that was not the most bizarre thing about her current predicament.

They were all staring at her and smiling, and the room was suddenly silent. The music had stopped and it was eerily quiet, there was no chatter, nothing at all. It was as though the whole world had paused before her eyes.

Charlotte panicked.

Have I interrupted a performance? She wondered as she stepped back.

"I'm so sorry," she said, flustered. "I'll just go out this way, I'm so..."

No one was moving. They were not letting her leave. She didn't know what to do.

Over the speakers, the unmistakable chimes of Mariah Carey's "All I Want For Christmas" began to play, and the people surrounding her all began to sing along.

Charlotte moved into the open, centre space so she was not in their way. She felt dizzy as she turned, watching them all dance in unison around her to a perfectly choreographed routine all directed at her.

"What's going on?" she asked as she spied the store manager among a group of observers who had gathered in a small audience, all grinning at the show before them. Was this a skit? A television documentary? The only cameras among the crowd of dancers or in the audience behind them were smart phones being held above heads, by people who were just as confused as she was.

A man stepped forward, separating himself from the dancers. He was wearing a red Santa hat and long white beard, but that was as far as his commitment to looking like Father Christmas went as his long, black Parka coat showed a very trim figure. As he pulled down his beard and smiled at her, there was a twinkle in his eye. He stepped closer, and closer, slowly reaching her and she realised she had stopped breathing. She knew this man. She knew him very well.

"Sam?" Charlotte was confused.

"Merry Christmas Charlotte."

"What are you doing?" she looked around, all eyes were still on her. As she turned back to Sam, he had lowered himself onto one knee.

"All I want for Christmas is youuuu," the dancers finished their routine and the music drifted back into the usual Christmas song list as the audience applauded and finally dispersed. Sam then pulled a small box from his pocket. He opened it and inside was a beautiful, platinum band with a square diamond on top.

"What are you doing? You can't…"

She tried to step back but Sam reached out and grabbed hold of her hand.

"Charlotte," he began. "When I saw you the other week, I didn't know what I would think. I didn't know what you'd be like with me. I had been so horrible to you. But seeing you, you looked amazing. You *do* look amazing. You were right about everything. I had a lot of changes I needed to make, and I've done it. I've done it all for you. I knew I wanted to propose, and there was only one way to do it. A flash mob, like I promised all those years ago. Do you remember?"

"I… I remember."

"So, Charlotte Hicks, I have to ask, will you marry me?"

Charlotte looked around her and a small crowd was still watching their interaction, including the store manager who was wiping tears from her eyes. A few of the observers were still filming them with their phones. It was then that Charlotte noticed where they were stood. They were at the back of the store, where seven months previous, chairs had been put out for her to meet L. Rosebud in person. And where she first laid eyes on Ross.

"Why don't we nip outside to a bench and talk?" she suggested.

"Erm," Sam didn't know what to say, still down on one knee. "Do you... do you want to answer the question first?"

"I think we need to talk first, let's go outside."

"Okay," he stood up and his face burned red. "What about the café instead?"

"No," Charlotte didn't want the connotation of this conversation in her favourite café. "We should get some air."

"I thought this was what you wanted?" Sam fiddled with the small box which was still in his hands.

Sam's disappointment was clear to anyone who walked past, even if they hadn't been privy to the interaction inside.

"It was, once upon a time." Charlotte was facing him as they sat beside each other on a bench, but he refused to look at her, keeping his eyes firmly on the ground. "I needed you to change, and you did. You should be so proud of that. But it was too late."

"Is there someone else?" he raised his voice this time, lifting his head.

"No. Not really. I tried to date someone, but I wasn't ready. He's gone now anyway."

"So, I did all this for nothing?" He put the ring box away in his pocket and finally faced her.

"No, not nothing. You needed to do it for yourself. I changed, look at me, but I did it for myself, no one else."

"I can't believe this," he shook his head and swore out loud.

"I'm sorry, I just…"

"No, not that. Them." He pointed to the store. "Bloody filming us in there. It'll be all over Facebook and TikTok. I've got an image to maintain now. My clients will see it and laugh at me. How could you do this to me?" he stood up.

"Do what? I didn't exactly know this was what you had planned. You can't blame me. How could I have known you'd do this? I wouldn't want you feeling embarrassed."

"Well I am, thanks a bunch."

The old Sam she had last seen on her birthday weekend was making himself known again. Charlotte knew then she had made the right decision. It was one thing to change how he looked, and to finally have a career doing what he was good at and could enjoy, but deep down, no one ever really changes that much.

Sam was standing by the bench with his back to Charlotte.

"When's the tenancy on the flat up?"

"Erm," Charlotte racked her brain. "February, I think."

"I'll carry on paying half the rent until then, but after that I'm stopping. If you want to stay there you can pay for it yourself."

"I wouldn't have expected you–"

"I think I've got everything of mine out of there already, but if there's anything left, just bin it." He buttoned the top button of his coat.

"I don't think there's–"

"Goodbye, Charlotte."

Sam walked away, not looking back. Charlotte watched him as he left.

Closure. Now she knew what that was.

CHAPTER 40

*D*avid spun Charlotte around the dance floor as the band played "Jai Ho" from the stage which was filled with singers, dancers and musical instruments of all kinds. The atmosphere was electrifying as the colourful lights above flashed around the room. No one was sitting, even Mrs Patel was letting loose on the dance floor, dragging Mr Patel around with her to the beat. Her smile was ear to ear as she could finally relax now the wedding was over and everything had gone smoothly. Her eldest child was married and happy, what more could she want?

Hema and Mark were in the centre of the dance floor in each other's arms, looking incredibly happy but also relieved that it was all over and they could look forward to their honeymoon in Vegas which, if Mrs Patel asked, you were instructed to lie about and say they were in Cumbria.

"How are you doing?" David shouted to Charlotte.

"I'm all right," she said as they continued dancing together. The lights above them gave off so much heat that they both had trickles of sweat on their foreheads. Everyone did, but it didn't matter. The room was filled with joy. "I've had the best day. I'm so pleased for them."

"Do you want to get some air?" David stood still, the heat was finally getting to him.

She nodded and he grasped her hand, pulling her away from the crowd and out into the gardens. There were twinkly fairy lights around every doorframe and window. Benches were situated along the path but he led her to the furthest one away where it would be quietest. Some of the guests outside couldn't help but dance along to the music and had turned the patio into an outdoor dance floor.

"Are you having a good time?" Charlotte asked.

"Amazing time," he leaned back on the bench and held out his arm and she leaned into him. "Feels good to let my hair down a bit."

"I'm so glad you could bring Ivy, she's done really well to last this long. It's almost midnight."

"Well, we brought everything apart from the cot with us. If she'd have been a bit older we'd have struggled I think. But at the moment all she wants to do is have some milk and then curl up into one of us. She's quite a content little thing."

"She's so beautiful, I'm so happy for you both. I'm so glad everything's worked out for you. And for Hema and Mark."

"And what about you? What are you going to do?"

"Here you both are," Matt found them and sat on the other side of Charlotte, leaving her sandwiched in the middle.

"Where's Ivy?" David asked, concerned.

"Don't worry. Hema's aunty Nisha, the one who sent all those knitted cardigans, insisted on having a hold so I could have a dance, but when I couldn't find either of you I assumed you'd be getting some air. Phew, it's warm in there. What are you guys talking about?"

"Charlotte, and what her plans are after Sam's surprising proposal but then not-surprising hissy fit before he spat his dummy out and stormed off."

"Well," Charlotte had to try defend him. "You can't blame him for being upset. I had just turned down his marriage proposal."

"Still, there's a dignified way to accept disappointment, and that wasn't it."

"Absolutely not," Matt agreed. "So, on the subject, have you decided what you're going to do?"

"I have," Charlotte smiled. "I've already started looking for a new apartment. I've given notice anyway. There are a few one-bedroom places not far from you actually. I've got some viewings arranged for January. They're affordable on a single wage."

"Excellent," David said. "That'll be good being so close by."

"Yeah, I've also sent a message to my boss to ask for a meeting in the new year. I want to see if I can amend my hours slightly, try to give myself some free time to focus on writing."

"Your work days are far too long as it is, no one can maintain doing that. It's ridiculous."

"Yeah, I'm going to suggest they promote Chloe, or at least give her a few more responsibilities. That'll free me up too. It's time I focused on me and my own dreams."

"And as for romance," Matt asked. "What are you going to do about that?"

Charlotte looked back at the venue and saw Hema and Mark making their way to them. Their arms were wrapped around each other. They were the very epitome of happiness and romance. It was a lovely picture, and seeing their two families come together to celebrate and combine two different cultures was truly heart-warming. She then thought to Matt and David, and how happy they were now their family was complete. So many different combinations of romance and happiness. Did she want that, of course, it would be lovely, but who was to say she couldn't be perfectly happy on her own?

"Well," she began. "You never know what could happen, do you?"

"Oh my God, guys, budge up. I need to sit down." Hema was

out of breath. Some strands of hair had come loose and were sticking to her cheeks. Mark had undone the top button of his shirt to let some cool air in.

"Here," Mark sat down first. "There isn't room for us all, sit down on my lap."

Mark squeezed onto the end and Hema sat on top of him.

"Well, you old married folk, how do you feel?" Charlotte asked.

"Hot. So very, very hot."

"I don't think I've ever danced that much," Mark said. "Nice and cool out here though."

A frost was creeping in around them. The sky was clear and the stars were glistening above them. They each took that moment to enjoy the peace. To enjoy the company around them. And to enjoy their upcoming Christmas as newlyweds for Hema and Mark, new parents for Matt and David, and newly single people like Charlotte.

What could the new year bring for them.

CHAPTER 41

JANUARY

The first day back at work after Christmas break was usually a long one, but this particular Monday was going to be different. The scheduled meeting between Charlotte and her boss was taking place that morning, and she was anxious of the outcome. She had never put herself forward before with a request. She had always done as she was told and never complained, but if things were going to change and she was going to allow herself time to focus on her own happiness, this was her chance.

"I think they're here." Chloe peaked through the blind. "A car's just pulled up and it isn't one of the parents."

Charlotte joined her at the window and saw the silver Mercedes pull up next to her car.

"Yes, that's Anne. She's the area manager. And that," she nodded to the man getting out of the passenger side. "I think that's the director. I don't know why he's come."

"I've never seen him before, why would he be here?"

"I have no idea, but I feel sick." Charlotte put her hand to her stomach and stepped away from the window.

"You'll be fine, honestly. Go sit down. I'll go down and bring them up."

"Thank you."

Charlotte sat at her desk as Chloe left the room and went down to let them in. They had just installed new facial recognition cameras at the doors so staff wouldn't have to authorise parents' entries every time, but they knew the big bosses wouldn't be able to let themselves in as the old fob system had been removed.

She drank some water from her bottle and took some slow breaths, in and out, in and out, in and out. Whatever the outcome of this meeting, she wouldn't be any worse off than she was now.

Chloe tapped at the door.

"Come in," Charlotte called as Chloe led Anne and the director inside. "Thank you, Chloe."

"Can I get you all anything? Tea or coffee?" Chloe asked.

"No, thank you, dear," Anne said. "We've just had one at the office."

Chloe left the room and Charlotte motioned at them to sit down. She had spent the morning cleaning the office so it looked presentable and setting out some chairs, pleased that she'd put a few out seeing as the director was there too.

"It's so nice to see you, Charlotte. It's been such a long time. You remember Mr Barrow, I think you've met."

"It was a while ago I think," Mr Barrow leaned forward and shook Charlotte's hand. "Possibly around when you interviewed for the manager position."

"Oh yes I think you're right."

"Well," Anne started. "There's a reason I've brought Mr Barrow along with me. I showed him your email and request and we thought we'd come and see you in person."

"Okay," Charlotte felt her cheeks go pink. Was this a good thing? Was she in trouble for making demands? Was this going to turn into a disciplinary?

"Yes, Charlotte," Mr Barrow said. "We had a quick meeting this morning. You want to reduce your hours I see. I questioned this, as your contract states you work forty hours, which is standard."

"And then we logged onto the portal," Anne jumped in. "To check the timesheets. We never check them, as we trust all of our managers to do their contracted hours. And as for the staff, managers keep on top of those anyway, so we've never had to check."

"But when we checked yours," Mr Barrow continued. "We saw some weeks, you'd been doing fifty hours, sometimes more."

"And not once had you submitted any requests to be paid for your overtime."

"We decided we couldn't have that. We don't want any of our staff feeling overworked. That's how you lose the good ones. And we don't want to lose you."

"Absolutely not," Anne said. "Look at this place. It's thriving because of you."

"So," Mr Barrow leaned forward. "Like we said, we had a meeting this morning. Spoke with our finance department too. We are going to backpay any overtime you did in the last twelve months. Unfortunately we couldn't backdate it any more."

"Oh my goodness," Charlotte finally spoke. "That's... that's amazing. I never would have expected that."

"And what's more, we are going to reduce your hours, but we're going to leave that up to you. How many hours are you thinking? If you want to keep your contract at forty hours per week, but then actually stick to forty hours a week, we'd be happy to do that. Fifty hours plus is far too much. But if you want to do less, let's have a think about it and I'm sure we could work something out."

Charlotte had thought about it a lot. She knew how many she wanted to do. She had even worked out how much she would earn and that she could still afford an apartment on a single wage. She'd noticed her outgoings had reduced a lot since living on her own.

"Well, I was thinking maybe if I did thirty-six hours, but over four days."

"Four days?" Anne asked.

"Yes, I could still do open and close those four days, but then it would free me up one day to pursue other ventures. Give me some time to myself, spend time with my niece. I think that's what I want to do."

"Okay, we hear you." Anne and Mr Barrow looked at each other. "We did discuss possibly bringing in another manager to help share the load. I don't know what you think about that."

"I think the workload is fine, I've certainly managed until now, however I know Chloe is keen to take on more responsibilities. She's helped me out a lot over the last twelve months. I think you'd be wise to consider her for some kind of promotion."

"Well," Mr Barrow spoke directly to Anne, as though Charlotte wasn't in the room. "I guess if we let Charlotte off one day a week, this Chloe could step up as the manager. If she wants to. Her paygrade could change for that one day."

"We'd probably have to put her up a paygrade anyway, if she's trained up properly. And then, if we're ever short at another nursery another day, we'd have her on hand in case we need last minute cover."

"She'll know some of the procedures already, saves bringing in someone new."

Charlotte allowed them some time to discuss it between themselves as she thought to how much she could achieve if she had a day off each week. A contracted day off. The amount of writing she could do. The day trips she could have. Even if she had a day to herself, it would make such a difference.

"Charlotte," Anne pulled her from her daydream. "We're going to seriously consider your offer. We'll go back to the office and speak with HR. Can we let you know sometime this week?"

"Of course, that's fine. Are you sure you don't want a drink?"

"No, thank you, we'll head off and start working something out. But, before we go," Anne paused. "Do you think we could meet Chloe again. Maybe she could show Mr Barrow around."

Charlotte realised it was so they could see Chloe in action.

"Of course," she said. "I'll go get her."

As Charlotte arrived home, she felt exhausted. She'd decided not to tell Chloe the full details of her request to the managers. She knew Chloe was more than ready for a promotion. Charlotte always trusted the nursery was in safe hands with Chloe around to support her. She deserved the opportunity.

Charlotte took her coat off to hang up, almost forgetting her phone was in the pocket. When she pulled it out she saw a text message from Hema.

> Hey! On our way to the airport. Mum still thinks we're off to Cumbria and has packed us loads of Tupperware filled with food! LOL! We've stuck it in the freezer. Not sure we'd get those through customs! If you've still got a key to our place, go help yourself! I'll message you when we're there. Place your bets now! Xxxx

> Have the best time! I've had a mad day, will save it for your return. Hopefully good things happening… and Red 12! Xxx

Charlotte saw another notification on her phone. This time, it was her emails.

Dear Charlotte,

Thank you for your enquiry. We are pleased to show you

Apartment 12, Upper Acre Building on West Mores Street tomorrow at 17:30.

Our agent Alistair will meet you there.

Kindest Regards

W. M. Properties

Apartment 12, it was a sign.

CHAPTER 42

"Feel free to have a look around," Alistair said after he had given her a tour. "I'll wait outside. Take your time."

"Thank you," she said, smiling. "I'll try not to take too long."

Alistair left her alone in the apartment and Charlotte made her way around once more, this time unaccompanied.

The ground floor apartment was perfect. The kitchen was small, which was fine for a single person, but there was room for a small dining table which is what she wanted. The lounge would be big enough for her current sofa suite, and the long back wall would be enough room for her bookcases, which pleased her. And there were two patio doors which led out onto a small, private garden area, just for her use. No more sharing and fighting to use the washing line in summer.

She wandered back down to the bedroom, which was possibly the largest room in the whole place. Her bed would go perfectly under the window and there was more than enough room for her desk and reading chair too. The built-in wardrobe was large enough for all her clothes. Next to them was the door to the ensuite, which didn't have a bath, just a shower, which didn't bother her either.

Back out on the landing was another door which opened up to a large storage area. There was hardly any storage space in the current apartment, she thought, so this would be very useful.

Charlotte knew she wanted it, but with the price being what it was, and with the great location too, she knew she'd have to be quick. She found Alistair outside. The apartment also had allocated parking, with enough spaces for visitors too in case anyone came to see her there.

"Well," he smiled at her. "What do we think?"

"I love it. It's perfect. When will it be ready?"

"Not long, couple of weeks. We've asked the landlord to authorise a deep clean which may take a week or two. So, you like it?"

"Yes, definitely." It was less than a mile to Matt and David's house too. "How do I sign up for it?"

"Well, I'll give you this form to register your interest, however, we have a few people wanting to have a viewing. I've got a couple booked in to see it right after you."

"Oh, right." She tried to hide her disappointment. "When will I find out?"

"Probably this week," he said confidently as he handed her the paper. "The landlord wants to get a move on with it. They don't like them being empty too long, so shouldn't be too long at all." He passed Charlotte a pen. "If you want to fill it out now I can take it back with me. Save you having to call in."

Charlotte took the paper back inside and leaned on the kitchen worktop to fill in her details. She took the chance to have another quick look around. There weren't many apartments like this around, and with her tenancy up soon, she knew she couldn't afford to renew it on her own. She had to have this apartment...

❧

"You could move in here with us if you need to stay somewhere," David suggested as Matt dished up their tea. Wine was not on the menu tonight seeing as though they had a sleepy Ivy in the bedroom, so Vimto was poured into tumblers.

"No I couldn't, you don't need the hassle. I have too many things anyway, there isn't enough room."

"It wouldn't be permanent," David said. "We could look into a storage unit for your furniture and other things. But if you're stuck while you find somewhere there's enough room here."

"Definitely," Matt said. "Don't be wasting any more money on that place if you don't need to. We have a spare room here if you need something temporary."

"That's so nice of you both," Charlotte said. "Thank you." Charlotte knew it would solve a problem, and she was grateful. "This apartment though, I'm in love with it already. I know you shouldn't go for the first place you look at, but everything about it is perfect. And it'll be all mine. Just mine. My own space."

"Hmm," David began. "Sounds like you need a cat."

Charlotte laughed.

"Don't be mean," Matt said. "She doesn't need a cat. She needs her new, reduced hours at work. Her shiny new apartment. And plenty of time to be herself, work on her book."

"Exactly," Charlotte agreed. "This is the year of me."

"Cheers to that."

They all raised their glasses of Vimto and clinked their glasses.

CHAPTER 43

riday took too long to arrive for Charlotte. It was almost the end of her work day and she still had not heard back from Anne about her job, or from Alistair about the apartment. She had hoped she would know by now what the future held for her, but it was not to be.

At midday, some of the part-time toddlers and children were picked up and the afternoon bunch arrived. Charlotte allowed Chloe to do the rounds to make sure everyone arrived happy and healthy, deciding to stay hidden in the office, waiting to hear about her fate.

When she heard a phone buzz, she got excited thinking it might be an email from the estate agent, but it was a voice note from Hema instead.

"Charlotte! You won't believe it, you won! I put a dollar on your number 12 and you won! That's twenty-five dollars. Not a lot, but still, yay! You're a good omen, speak soon, love ya!"

At least that's something, she thought.

Five minutes later, the office phone rang.

"Charlotte, it's Anne, how are you doing?"

"I'm good thanks, how are you?"

"Oh good, all good thanks. I'm so sorry it's taken this long to get back to you. You know how it is when you try do things with HR. A five-minute job ends up taking three days, ha, it's the same everywhere. Anyway, I have good news."

❧

Charlotte danced down the stairs from the office in search of Chloe. She found her in Bananas calming an upset baby boy. It was one of the new admissions, still getting used to the transition of being handed over to the nursery staff and watching his mum walking away.

"Chloe," she said calmly so as not to upset the baby. "When you've got a moment, can you come up to the office?"

"Yes, course, I won't be long."

"Thank you."

Charlotte couldn't wait to tell her the news.

When Chloe finally arrived, her shoulder wet from the baby's tears, she closed the door and sat in the seat opposite Charlotte.

"Are you okay?" Chloe asked. "Have you found out anything yet?"

"Anne just called, and they've authorised my request."

"That's amazing! Aw wow, well done you. You must be thrilled."

"I am," she beamed. "I can't believe it. It's not going to affect my pay by much really, and with the backdated payment for overtime I'll be sorted for a bond and rent in advance when I finally move somewhere new."

"I'm so happy for you, you deserve this after all you've been through."

"Thank you, but there's more." Charlotte stood and got the document from the printer which Anne had sent across after their conversation. "This is for you, they want to know if you'd like a promotion."

"A… a promotion?" Chloe took the paperwork and read over the new contract details. "This is… they want me as manager? Really?"

"Yes," Charlotte said. "They need someone they can trust to cover on the day I won't be working, and to be on hand if another nursery needs cover. You really impressed them when they visited. So they want to offer you the position, give you first refusal, and if you don't want it they can advertise it. But don't rush, okay? Think it over. Honestly though, you could do this job blindfolded."

"You really think so?" Chloe asked.

"Yes, and in my opinion, there's no one else I'd have working alongside me."

When Charlotte was locking up the nursery that evening, she had a spring in her step. Even though she hadn't heard about the apartment, she got the news she'd been waiting for about her job. There would be other apartments, she was sure about that.

As she walked across the car park, her phone rang.

"Charlotte, it's Alistair, how are you doing?"

"Alistair, hi. I'm great thanks."

"Good, good. I'm sorry it's taken me all week to call you back. The first week after the Christmas holidays is always a busy one catching up with viewings. But I have news. The apartment is yours if you still want it?"

She stood still as she had finally approached her car, not sure she had heard him correctly.

"Hello?"

"Sorry," Charlotte said. "Sorry, I didn't think I heard you right then. The apartment is mine?"

"Yes, if you'd still like it. We send the applications to the landlord to check over for themselves. A few people actually pulled out, said there wasn't really enough room for a couple to live in. The landlord didn't want to risk some people moving in and then deciding they wanted somewhere bigger and for it to be empty again in six months. So, if you're interested in a long-term let, the landlord would like to offer it to you. What do you think?"

"Alistair, I think you've just made my day."

"So that's a yes?"

"Yes. A thousand times yes. You have no idea how happy I am right now."

"Wonderful. It'll actually be ready from Monday. The cleaning has been done already so it's good to go. Just depends how soon you want to get in there."

"As soon as humanly possible, Alistair."

"Brilliant! Well, we're closing up now, but if you'd like to call into the office in the morning we can look over the contracts. It's a short day with it being Saturday, so if you could come around ten or eleven? Would that be okay?"

"Ten is great, I'll see you then."

CHAPTER 44

*C*harlotte piled the boxes high on top of one another. It took nine large plastic containers to hold just her books. She wouldn't be able to lift them herself, so had arranged a removal company to come and help her move into her new apartment. When she spoke to Anne to confirm Chloe would be thrilled to take on the position, she also told her about the move, and Anne had allowed her to book some annual leave at short notice so she had enough time to pack up and move without worrying about work. Everything was happening so quickly, which was what Charlotte needed to kickstart the new year.

The time had finally come. It was her last night in the apartment she'd taken on with Sam. Her life with him, the good and the bad, seemed like a lifetime ago. She kept seeing ads for his web design business popping up every now and then. It looked like he was doing well for himself, and she was genuinely pleased for him.

Charlotte spent the whole evening packing, almost forgetting about tea. She decided that her last night there meant she needed something quick and easy.

She opened the Just Eat app on her phone. She hadn't used it for so long it needed an update before it would allow her in. She found one of the old, favourite Chinese takeaways and ordered herself a mini feast. It wouldn't do any harm, she thought. Not with the amount of calories she'd burned that week packing and carrying boxes. Her living room was no longer a place to relax, but a place to carefully step so you didn't trip and fall into a pile of boxes, suitcases filled with clothes, or rubbish bags destined for the tip. They were ready for collection the next day.

Her Chromebook was still at her desk. That would be last to be packed. Any chance she got, she was switching it on and adding more and more to her story. She still had the handwritten plan which she couldn't bear to throw away. Not when it had Ross' notes written among the madness.

She decided to look on Amazon to see if his new book was on there yet, available to pre-order. It was this time the previous year she had pre-ordered his last book.

There it was.

"The Safe Goodbye" by L. Rosebud.

Release date 15th March

Available to pre-order now

Charlotte still had the copy of the manuscript he had given her of this very book, but she couldn't bring herself to read it. It had been safely packed away among her other books to be read one day. She didn't know when. All of the L. Rosebud books fit into their own box. She owned every single one. They were all the same size, paperback copies and sat together nicely on the bookcase. It would be wrong not to own this latest book in the same format, she thought. So she clicked to pre-order. Another year, another birthday treat to herself.

Luckily, realisation that she was moving the next day hit and she very quickly updated her address information so it would be delivered to the correct place.

Charlotte heard her phone ringing from the other room. She

assumed it would be her takeaway confirming the order and that they were on their way, but it was Hema.

"Hey, I'm just checking in on how you're doing?"

"I'm good, it's kind of sad, but I'm good. Just about ready I think. When did you get back?"

"Just this morning," Hema yawned. "Mark's in bed. He was throwing up on the plane home."

"Oh no!"

"Yeah, that was gross. He was *not* popular. I pretended not to know him."

"You sound like a very sympathetic wife." Charlotte laughed.

"Oh I am, I am. I'm doing my best to stay as far away from him as possible so I don't catch his yucky illness too. I'd have come straight over to help you out but I don't want to pass it on to you either."

"Ah that's fine, I'm happy just hanging out on my own. I've ordered a takeaway, everything is pretty much ready to go. I've got the keys to the new place. Bring on tomorrow."

"What time are the movers coming?"

"Not until nine," Charlotte looked out the window and saw some headlights pulling down the road. "No rush then. I think my food's here."

"Okay, I'll let you go, call me if you need anything. If you're free next weekend let's go shopping, yeah?"

"That sounds like a plan, we'll sort something out."

"Okay, enjoy your last night, bye!"

CHAPTER 45

The Trafford Centre was nicely quiet that following weekend. The January Sale madness was over and the shopping community were in their February lull. This suited Charlotte and Hema who wanted to take their time looking around the shops. Hema wanted new clothes and Charlotte wanted to look at décor for her new apartment. Her old sofa suite was fine but it was a bit of a squeeze, so she had ordered a new one from DFS and now was on the hunt for cushions and throws to accessorise. She also wanted new bedding, a rug, and many more things to make her first apartment alone her very own personal space, with only the things that she selected herself without the need to negotiate with anyone else.

"What about this?" Hema pointed to a grey, faux-rabbit fur rug. "This is so snug. Imagine this under your feet as you get out of bed. What do you think?"

"Oh I love it," Charlotte ran her hands through the fur. "So soft. Where's the tag? Oh look, it's still in the sale. And it's the last one. Let's pop it in the basket before someone else takes it. Are you all right?"

Hema was standing a few steps away from her with her hand over her mouth and her eyes closed.

"Yes," she struggled to speak. "It's… it's that bug Mark had. It's made its way over to me I think."

"Do you want to go home? I can pay for this quickly and we can head off."

"No," she shook her head. "No, I just need a drink. If we head to the food court you can get your lunch, I'll just grab a bottle of water or something."

"Okay, if you're sure, I don't mind leaving."

"No, it'll pass. I'm sure."

They made their way to the selection of restaurants. Hema found a table to wait at with their shopping bags whilst Charlotte got herself a sandwich with a hot chocolate, and a bottle of water for her sickly friend. Although, she was suspicious of this illness. Mark's vomiting episode turned out to be food poisoning, and even so, that was over a week ago.

"Here's your water." She joined Hema at the table who seemed a lot more relaxed now she was sat down.

"Thank you." Hema opened the bottle and took small sips which seemed to make her feel better.

"So," Charlotte began, trying but failing to hide a smile. "Is this a delayed reaction to food poisoning or what?"

There could never be any secrets between the two best friends. Their eyes possessed powers to convey an entire conversation without actually speaking. And Hema's eyes made the confession with just a few seconds of Charlotte's knowing stare.

"Oh my God, Charlotte, please don't tell anyone yet."

"You are then?"

"Yes," she finally smiled too. "I'm pregnant."

"Oh my God, that's so exciting! But wait, this is good news, why can't we tell anyone?"

"Think about it…" she whispered. "Clearly I was pregnant *at* the wedding."

"Ah, Mrs Patel."

"Yes, so as far as anyone is concerned, mine and Mark's baby is due to arrive prematurely in around seven months' time."

"Seven months, premature, got it. As long as you don't give birth to a nine pounder then you should get away with that story."

"I'd hope it wouldn't weigh that much anyway." She managed a laugh, but was hit with another wave of nausea. "What's in that sandwich?"

"It's just ham, nothing too pungent." Charlotte had purposely picked it thinking, if her suspicions were correct, it would be safe around someone with morning sickness.

"I need chips."

"Sorry?" Hema's random request caught her off guard.

"Chips. McDonald's chips. Don't ask me why, I've had a thing for salty food lately, it just works somehow."

Charlotte stood quickly. "Wait right there, mama, I'll go get some. Anything else?"

"No, just chips. Very salty chips."

"Coming right up."

Hema polished off a large portion of McDonald's chips and, as if they contained magical powers, she was ready to continue shopping. It was several hours until they were done, with bags and bags to negotiate between them to take back to Charlotte's car.

"Eurgh, Valentine's Day," Hema said as they walked past a card shop.

"You sound like a very happy newlywed, I must say."

"I don't need Valentine's anymore, I'm married. What about you? Is there any romance going on I should know about?"

"No, none at all. Although…"

Charlotte told Hema that she had pre-ordered Ross' new book and it was due to arrive on her birthday like the year before.

"I don't see a problem with that," Hema reassured her friend. "It might be Ross' book, but L. Rosebud is a different entity entirely. You can still enjoy his books like you did before. You were in a relationship with the author long before Ross came along. Have you unpacked your books yet?"

"No," Charlotte admitted. "I haven't got around to that yet. I'll find the time, I'll do it."

"I can come help if you want?"

"No, it's fine. I'll get to it. Might as well wait until the new sofa comes anyway, that shouldn't be long."

"What do you think of your new apartment so far? I know you've barely been in a week, but does it feel like home yet?"

"Do you know what?" Charlotte said. "It really does."

CHAPTER 46

*C*harlotte spent the rest of her weekend organising and accessorising her new apartment. There was an unseasonable warmth in the air so she quickly washed her brand-new bedding so she could get it hung outside to dry in her own garden. She decided she would need to visit the local garden centre that spring and buy some bedding plants for the first time ever. There were some empty pots left by the previous tenants she could use and fill with the most colourful flowers like pansies or violas. By the evening, the bedding was dry and ready to go on her bed. She smoothed down the duvet and then placed her new throw neatly across the bottom.

Deciding it was time to tackle the books, she unloaded them one box at a time, stacking them in the living room until every book she owned was piled up, grouped together by genre. The romance books dominated the space, with the horror, crime and odd non-fiction book there too. And then, the final box contained the L. Rosebud books. All nineteen of them, with the twentieth due out in just a few weeks. Hema was right, Charlotte decided. L. Rosebud the author was a different entity to Ross the person. There was no reason she couldn't still enjoy the books, and give them pride of place.

One by one, in chronological order, Charlotte placed them gently on their own shelf within the bookcase. The older ones stood out with their creased spines from being read over and over again. She found *Wish Upon Your Heart,* which Ross has signed for her the previous year. She ran her hand across the cover and flipped it open and read the first paragraph. She could hear his voice reading it back to her. In her mind, she could see his lips moving as he read each word. She felt sad she would never see him again. That she had ruined the chance to be with someone like Ross. Someone mature, caring, encouraging, handsome, funny. It was bad timing, she knew that, but how she wished it wasn't.

It took Charlotte two hours to organise her books how she wanted. The entire wall was filled with literature for all to see, and not hidden away in a spare room. By Sunday morning the living room was looking a lot more like home. She sat down on the sofa with a cup of tea and toast when she heard a knock at the door.

"Bugger," she said to herself as she tightened her dressing gown and went to see who it was.

"Delivery, love." The courier said as he handed over a big bouquet of beautiful colourful flowers.

"Thank you." She looked them over. "Are you sure they're for me?"

"Hicks?" he answered impatiently.

"Yes, that's me."

"Then they're for you." He turned to walk away without another word.

"Thanks," she called after him, thinking he'd be more suited to delivering bailiff letters rather than flowers.

Charlotte closed the door and checked the small card sticking out of the flowers.

> To Aunty Charlotte,
> I hope you like your new home. I can't wait to visit. Please can you join my daddies and me for brunch next weekend?
> Love From
> Ivy xxx

Charlotte smiled at the sweet request. She brought the flowers into the kitchen and searched for something to put them in. It had been quite a while since she'd had some flowers on display so unpacking the box containing the vase hadn't been a priority.

A glass would have to suffice as a temporary measure, she decided, so put them in the largest glass she had available and put them on the windowsill before sending a quick text message to her brother.

> Please tell Ivy I absolutely adore the flowers and that I would love to join you all for brunch. Just let me know where/when and I'll be there xxx

> Ivy is pleased you like them – she chose them herself! Brunch at our place next Sunday from 11am. Hema and Mark coming too xxx

> Wonderful, I'll be there xxx

> Great, what are you up to? Fancy coming for a stroll with us at the park? Xxx

Actually I need to finish up here as much as I can. Back to work tomorrow so want to get the kitchen organised etc xxx

Okay, will let you get on 😊 speak soon xxx

Charlotte put her phone down and it pinged again. This time with an email.

Meet the author!
Dear Customer,
We thought you'd be interested to know that L. Rosebud is returning to bookstores
nationwide as part of the release of The Safe Goodbye
As you confirmed attendance last year, we would like to offer you the opportunity
to secure your place in advance at your nearest store.
Click here <> to book your place now.
Regards
Bloomfield Publishers

Without any hesitation, Charlotte clicked the link to see and there it was. He would be returning to her local Waterstones store on 15 March. On the day the book comes out. Charlotte's birthday.

CHAPTER 47

"*How* ow did you get on last week?" Charlotte asked Chloe once all the babies and children were settled into their rooms and the parents had left.

"Really well," she said. "It's the first time I've been in charge on my own for a whole week, but it was great. Anne came out to see me on Tuesday to get my signed contract. She talked about my paygrade increase too and when that's effective from. Apparently I'm going on a two week course in Leeds over the summer to learn about the finance and legal side of things."

"Ah yes, I did that. It's not the most exciting two weeks of your life, but it's handy stuff to learn. Also, it means the nursery's insurance is covered in case of a major disaster when you're in charge."

"Oh great, that fills me with confidence," they both laughed. "I'll go check on the rooms. Do you want to come with me?"

"No," Charlotte said. "You go. I've got a week of emails to catch up on. Tell them I'll be down this afternoon to read stories to them."

Chloe left the office and Charlotte opened her inbox.

There were the usual junk emails from children's

educational toy manufacturers wanting them to place an order. A few new parent enquiries which she would reply to that day to arrange nursery viewings. There were also a few Amazon recommendations for books relating to childcare, gentle parenting and weaning. There was one email she kept going back to though, but this one was on her personal email account.

Meet the author.

Charlotte still hadn't decided whether or not to go. Would she be welcome? Would Ross be pleased to see her? Would it be too uncomfortable for him and therefore ruin his author event? She had no idea. She needed a second opinion. She knew she'd get that opinion, as well as a few more, that weekend at her brother's brunch. They would all know what was best for her.

Her phone started ringing which made her jump, pulling her out of her dilemma.

"Hello?"

"Hello, is that Charlotte?" a male voice asked.

"Yes, speaking." She expected it to be a sales call that she would soon be hanging up on.

"Hi, it's Alistair."

The estate agent, she remembered, assuming he'd be calling to check up on how everything was going on with the apartment.

"Hello, Alistair, how's it going?"

"Good, splendid, good. How are you finding the apartment?"

"It's all wonderful, thank you. I'm settling in. It's really quiet at the moment, no noisy neighbours, so I can't complain at all so far. I figured out the central heating. Took me a while but I got it in the end."

"Good, good. That's really good."

"Is there anything I can help you with?" Charlotte said to break up the awkward silence which followed his last words.

"Well, actually," he stuttered. "I, erm. I just wondered, erm… If you erm… would like to get a drink with me some time?"

This time, it was Charlotte's turn to throw an awkward silence into the mix.

"Oh..." was all she managed to get out.

"Yes I just thought when I saw you, you were really pretty, seemed really nice, and with moving in on your own I just assumed... I mean well, I don't want to sound rude, but I assumed you were single. And I, well, I really liked you and figured, you know, you never really know unless you just go for it. So... what do you think?"

It was the last thing she was expecting to hear. She was glad he'd called her rather than visit as, even though she was on her own, her face was burning.

"Alistair, I am really flattered. Truly, I am. But, I'm afraid its just not the right time for me to be going out for drinks with you. Or anyone, for that matter."

"Ah yes, I understand, I'm sorry for–"

"Please don't be sorry. You have no idea how much I probably needed to hear that. But I am sorry. Thank you, though."

"I'm glad I could, erm, tell you something you needed to hear. Goodbye."

Charlotte hung up, totally surprised by that call.

She wondered about what he said though. "You never really know unless you just go for it."

He was right, she thought. You never do know unless you just do it.

CHAPTER 48

he sun was still shining when her Sunday brunch date arrived, so Charlotte left her car in her allocated parking spot and walked the one mile to Matt and David's house. There were still hints of frost in the shaded areas, but it had already melted where the sun was touching. Charlotte wrapped up, feeling the chill in the air, wearing her long winter coat with faux fur around the hood and her favourite grey Dorothy Perkins scarf wrapped around her neck keeping her warm, tucked inside her coat to give her some insulation. She hadn't been able to find her gloves yet, which were still hidden in one of the boxes she'd shoved in the storage space, so she let her hands take cover in the sleeves.

When she walked up Matt's driveway, she saw Hema's car was already there. She was excited to see her friend, and wondered if the pregnancy had been officially announced yet so they could have a little celebration.

"Hello?" Charlotte let herself in the front door.

"Hello, hello," Matt called from the conservatory. "Come through, we're in here."

Charlotte walked in to see four adults crouched on the floor around a cooing, giggling baby Ivy.

"What's going on here?" she asked, taking off her coat and crouching down beside them.

"Hema and Mark brought an activity mat for Ivy," Matt said. "Look at her, she loves it."

Ivy was laid on her back, fascinated by the arch of colour above her with a dangling mirror, giraffe, zebra and lion.

"She's obsessed with looking at herself in the mirror," David said. "She's so my child."

They all laughed in agreement and one by one decided the floor was too painful to kneel down on for too long and took their places around the dining table which was filled with plates of sandwiches, pastries, chopped fruit and a Victoria sponge cake taking centre place. David had brought down his tea set and poured drinks into fancy cups which were sat atop their matching saucers. The days of afternoon drinking were clearly far behind them.

"How are you doing, Hema?" Charlotte asked, wanting to be mindful in case she ruined any surprise they were yet to announce.

"I'm fine," she said. "A lot better, anyway," she whispered. "We thought we'd let Matt and Dave know today. In fact..." she reached into her pocket and pulled something out. "Guys, when you're ready, Mark and I have an announcement."

"Oh, sounds ominous. Don't tell me you're getting divorced already." David laughed.

"No," Hema smiled. "No separation, more like an extension. Here." Hema opened her hand and revealed a scan photo of a tiny foetus.

"Oh my goodness!" Matt and David said together, getting up from their seats to offer hugs and congratulations.

"We were so surprised," Mark said.

"This is so exciting, Ivy is going to have a cousin," David said.

He picked Ivy up from her playmat. "Ivy, you're going to have a cousin, isn't that exciting? Oh," she started crying. "I don't think she wanted pulling away from the mirror." He gently laid her back down in her spot and the crying stopped once she saw her own face reflecting back at her. "You are *so* my child," he said again, almost proudly.

"And how's the morning sickness going?" Charlotte asked.

"Oh it's loads better now. Still have the odd moment, like yesterday when my mum brought in a pot of Earl Grey tea."

"Yes, that was quickly removed from the room. And then we had no choice but to share the news there too," Mark said.

"You told Mrs P?" Charlotte was surprised. "How did she take it, with the dates?"

"Oh fine, she thinks it's a honeymoon blessing, so it's totally acceptable. We still might need to be a little bit premature, but we should get away with it."

"I figure we should be safe though, it's the first grandchild after all," Mark said. "So, any wrath from figuring things out would be cancelled by general happiness and spoiling of them."

"Them?" Charlotte asked.

"Yes," Hema passed the scan photo to her. "Look. We're having twins."

The next hour of brunching was filled with talking about babies. Baby cries, nappies, poonamis, sleeping patterns, feeding, burping. The new parents were thrilled to be talking about their experiences with the soon-to-be parents. Telling them what to expect, what they would never expect, but mostly all the joy they would feel once their family was complete. That there was nothing better than watching your baby sleep.

"Charlotte," Hema said. "Are you all right? You've been quiet."

"Oh, yes I'm fine. Just listening to you guys." She smiled to try to hide how she was really feeling.

"Char, I'm so sorry. We've just been talking about babies."

"It's okay, Matt, really. Your lives are about babies now, you can't not talk about it just because I'm here and babyless."

David was now holding Ivy in his arms. She was asleep after finishing off a whole bottle of milk. "What is going on with you though? What's been happening?"

"Yeah, what's going on at work?" Mark asked.

"How's the new apartment? We need a house-warming party." Hema said.

Charlotte loved the idea of a party, but with her best friend off alcohol for a while, and with her brother now having parental duties, she figured it wouldn't be much of a party, not like the ones they were all used to. Times were changing.

"The new apartment is great, work is fine too. Loving my new reduced hours. Oh, I got asked out last weekend by my estate agent."

"You what? You never said. When are you going out?" Matt asked.

"Oh, no, I said no. I was incredibly flattered, he's called Alistair and he was lovely, but no. I didn't really feel up for that."

"Any more from Sam?" Hema asked.

"No," Charlotte said. "Sam is well and truly gone out and out of the picture, which I'm pleased to say. He may have changed his looks and attire, though nothing else about him changed. But…"

"But what?" Hema asked.

"I had this email," she opened the message on her phone and passed it around for them all to see. "I don't know what to do."

They each had a read through of the message detailing the author event.

"You have to go," Hema said. "You need to."

"I don't know," Matt said. "Your head was too messed up last year. I still think you need some more time."

"Sod waiting, get yourself there, hun," David said.

"I just don't know what to do. I think I want to see him. No, I do want to see him. But does he want to see me?"

"Did he not send the email?" Mark asked.

"No," Charlotte took her phone back. "It's an auto-generated thing because I signed up at last year's event. He won't know I've had it."

"Honestly, Charlotte," Hema began. "You can do one of two things. You can bite the bullet and call him now. Ask to meet up and talk to him. Or you could take the next month to really think about it and go to this event. You never know, he might want you to be there."

Alistair's words were still echoing around her mind. Should she just do it?

CHAPTER 49

15TH MARCH

*C*harlotte had not been back inside her local Waterstones ever since Sam's unexpected proposal. She would expect he'd never return there either after what happened, so there was no chance of bumping into him. Charlotte was pleased she never used social media anymore just in case the proposal did pop up on TikTok or Facebook for all to see.

She pushed the door open, pleased to see it was quiet. The manager was nowhere to be seen. There were still ten minutes until the event was due to begin, so Charlotte made a right, away from the romance section, just in case Ross would be lingering there again. She was hoping to sit at the back of the audience, hidden behind other heads, so she could listen to him speak, see his face, before deciding whether or not to make herself known.

Charlotte walked past tables with various books on display and she imagined her book being there one day. She now had a first draft completed, but had no idea what to do with it or where to send it. Could she send it to a publisher? Would she need an agent? Could she self-publish? She had so many questions, and they were questions she would need to ask a fellow writer, for advice.

As she made her way down the store, passing the infamously mortifying proposal area, she spied the chairs set up in the back. There were more than the previous year, which was a good sign. There must be a lot of people coming which meant it would be easy to hide in the back. Several people had taken their seats, but not enough yet for her to sit down herself, so she carried on pretending to look at the books around her, and then she saw him.

Ross had his back to her, but it was definitely him. Charlotte was nervous, but her excitement at seeing him again spoke volumes. She knew what she wanted.

"Charlotte," the manager found her. "What are you doing hiding back here? You'll want a front row seat, won't you?"

"Oh, erm, well, not quite. I'm going to sit at the back, just waiting for it to fill up a bit more."

"But why would you want to hide? Look, we all thought that proposal was a bit mad," the manager put a hand on Charlotte's shoulder. "But there's no need for *you* to be embarrassed."

"Actually it's not that…"

"Oh, it's time," she checked her watch. "Two minutes until it starts. I'd best get down there. Take your seat, and honestly, don't worry about it!" She waddled down to the platform.

Charlotte hung back for as long as she could, until finally, most of the seats were taken and she was able to slip into one of the back seats behind a very tall person, nicely blocking her view. Ross would not see her from here among all the faces.

"Good afternoon, everyone," the manager spoke into the microphone. "Welcome back, I see some faces who were here last year when L. Rosebud came to us for the first time." She smiled proudly. "We're so pleased to have him back and to promote his new book. I believe Mr Rosebud is going to give us a quick reading, and then answer some of your budding questions before taking his place over there," she gestured to a table and chair, "to sign your books. So, I am pleased to introduce, Mr L. Rosebud."

The store erupted into applause and cheers as he took his place by the microphone, smiling to the people gathered before him, but Charlotte noticed that the twinkle that had been in his eyes the previous year was not there anymore.

"Thank you, everyone. I am truly humbled at how many of you have come out to see me again." He seemed to be scanning the audience so Charlotte tilted her head out of sight. "Last year, I came here for the first time, and it was an experience I will never forget. When my publisher asked if I'd like to return, I couldn't refuse."

One of the women on the front row let out a "woo" and clapped.

"Thank you," he smiled at her. "I appreciate the enthusiasm."

He was definitely not the same, Charlotte thought. Something was wrong.

"Let's begin, here is a passage from my book which some of you may have pre-ordered for today. The manager assures me there were plenty requested from here which have arrived and been collected, so if you would like me to sign those, I will be more than happy." He cleared his throat and began reading from his book.

Charlotte was entranced, just like she had been the previous year, but there was a subtle difference in his tone. She looked around her and everyone was fixated on him. It was mostly women, but their smiles were ear to ear as they took in his every word. Charlotte wondered if it was just her who could see that there was a change in him.

Ross closed his book as he finished reading.

"Thank you so much for listening," he said. "I will now take a few questions, and then proceed to the signing."

Hands flew up around her.

"Yes, to the lady with the red plaited locks. What's your question?"

"Hi, Mr Rosebud," she stood. "I'm such a huge fan, I've read all of your books."

"Thank you," he smiled. "I'm flattered."

"My question to you, what would you say is the most romantic date?"

"Hmm, most romantic. Well, definitely something isolated where you can have a really good, in-depth conversation to really get to know each other. Maybe somewhere scenic where you could share a picnic whilst sitting on the grass taking inspiration from everything around you."

Like Bolton Abbey, Charlotte thought.

"Thank you for your question, is there anyone else…" a room full of hands shot up in the air. "Quite a few of you. Yes, the lady with the pink scarf."

"Hi, Mr Rosebud," she blushed. "I wanted to know, apart from romance, what books do you enjoy reading."

"A good question," he scratched his chin. "Well, I do generally stick to romance, but I do enjoy romantic comedy. They can be really funny if done correctly."

Like my book, Charlotte thought. Ross had said the market needed more romantic comedy like the one she was working on.

"Thank you. Yes, to the lady with the denim jacket. What's your question, please?"

"Hi, Mr Rosebud." Another lady stood up. "I know this book is only out today, but when do you think your next one will be out?"

"Well," he scratched his chin again. "Honestly I finished this book a few months ago. But I haven't actually got plans for another as yet. I know I usually have them on the go straight away, but I will be taking a short hiatus whilst I try and find some inspiration. I may even experiment with another genre for a change, but I'll see how things go."

I broke him, Charlotte thought.

"I might take one more question, are there any more?"

"Yes!" Charlotte shouted. "Here, please!"

"Someone is very eager to talk," he smiled. "Love the enthusiasm here today, yes, I can see a hand but I can't see a face. You can stand if you…"

Charlotte stood.

Ross was silent as their eyes locked together.

Everyone in the audience looked back and forth between them, wondering what was happening. Even the manager looked confused.

"Do…" Ross finally broke the silence. "Do you have a question?"

"Yes," Charlotte said. "Yes, I have a question. Possibly two, depending on the answer to the first."

"Okay," Ross' lip twitched as he tried to hold back a smile. "Let's have the first question, please."

"Have you ever been in love?"

There it was, Charlotte noticed. The sparkle in his eyes, making a subtle return.

"That's quite a question. I suppose, yes. I have." He didn't take his eyes from hers. "Love can be quite a tricky thing though. But yes, I know what love feels like, and I know how much it can hurt when you think you've lost it. But then, suddenly and unexpectedly, it can appear right before your eyes and you remember what it feels like." He smiled at her. "Does that qualify for a second question?"

"Yes," she smiled back at him, nodding her head, feeling every eye in the room upon her on the edge of their seats also waiting for the next question. "My next question, Mr *Rosebud*, is… would you like to get a coffee with me after this?"

All heads in the audience, and some spectators from the sides doing their book shopping, turned back to him, waiting for his answer.

"Well, I hear there is a nice café upstairs. Would you recommend it?"

There were murmurs among the audience now, with several people sharing their love of the famous Waterstones café.

"Absolutely. It's my favourite place. I was thinking of heading up there anyway. I'd love to have some company, if you're available."

"Well then," the sparkle had truly returned to his eyes as he spoke now. Charlotte couldn't help but blush as he smiled back at her. "How can I refuse? I would *love* to have a coffee with you."

THE END

ACKNOWLEDGEMENTS

I want to send my many, never ending thanks to everyone at Bloodhound Books. I am so grateful for all they have done and I hope to have many more books written for them in the future for you, my lovely readers, to enjoy.

ALSO BY DEBBIE IOANNA

Abberton House

Blind Date

A NOTE FROM THE PUBLISHER

Thank you for reading this book. If you enjoyed it please do consider leaving a review on Amazon to help others find it too.

We hate typos. All of our books have been rigorously edited and proofread, but sometimes mistakes do slip through. If you have spotted a typo, please do let us know and we can get it amended within hours.

info@bloodhoundbooks.com

Printed in Great Britain
by Amazon